And on the Eighth Day

And on the Eighth Day

J.T. HOLDEN

ISBN 13: 978-1-937696-37-5

for Tessa,
who, with a single word of kindness,
turned what I initially (and erroneously) believed to be
an irredeemable character into a hero.

for that boy who spoke only with his hands and his heart;
for the crack of the bat driving the ball over the fences;
for that first kiss under the bleachers as the ballpark
erupted with cheers that neither of us heard.

in loving memory of
Krystal Grace Brady, our sweet Faye-Faye,
who treated all her books with gentle care,
as if they were her own children.

"But thou art fair, and at thy birth, dear boy,
  Nature and Fortune join'd to make thee great."

— William Shakespeare

"Count your lucky stars,
  Count what you've been looking for.
  Oh boy, oh boy,
  Count the life you lead,
  Count how you are now adored."

— Ed Roland

one

If someone had told Jake Leary yesterday that, in less than twenty-four hours, he would be having a friendly chat over a couple of beers at a local gay pub with his straitlaced next-door neighbor, he would have laughed. Not only was Christian Worthing a staunch evangelical conservative, with a hard core anti-immigration stance and a firm belief that "the only thing that can stop a bad guy with a gun is a good guy with a gun," he also had a "Make America Great Again" bumper sticker on his Jeep Grand Cherokee, which all by itself was more than enough to keep Jake on his own side of the fence. That is, of course, until the fence in question was literally smashed down by a huge black elm during the worst storm ever recorded in the entire one hundred and twenty-nine-year history of Dante's Haven.

In the wake of that destructive early-autumn storm, which ushered in an unseasonable heat wave that would last for seven days before finally giving way to a cool northeastern breeze, everything changed.

And nothing would be the same again.

two

Jake stood on the wide front porch of his house, surveying the damage. It was bad, but not nearly as bad as the back lawn, which sloped down toward the lake, where twisted panels of aluminum siding and roof tiles floated on the calm surface like debris from a sunken ship. It was going to be a bitch cleaning it up. He briefly considered enlisting a couple of neighborhood teenagers to help with the cleanup and paying them fifty bucks each, which would be a bargain, considering the magnitude of the mess. But with a sad look at the devastation up and down Revelation Road, Jake was sure they'd all be busy cleaning up their own lawns. He figured the best he could do would be to take care of whatever cleanup he could manage on his own and then hire a professional crew to clear away the heavy stuff—the massive elm that had demolished the fence between his property and the Worthing's and the tall oak out back that had crushed his shed.

Jake started on the front lawn and had made decent progress by a quarter after eleven. His city-issued trash bin was full after only half an hour's work, and so he started stacking debris against the side of the garage. He noticed that a neighbor down the street had rented a large dumpster and made a mental note to get the company's name and number later. Some of the houses had taken severe damage—especially the ones whose owners had failed to secure their shutters before the storm had come whistling in off the northeast end of the lake. Shattered glass and mangled mullion slats littered the lawns of these houses, and angry-looking people were up on ladders, latching their shutters like farmers closing the barn doors *after* the livestock has escaped.

While Dante's Haven was a beautiful place to live—at least when the storm season had passed—it wasn't populated with cheery people. For the most part, residents kept to themselves and didn't bother with more than a nod and a grunt when they passed you on the street. And they certainly didn't have time for smart-guy gawkers watching them button up their shutters after their windows had been blown out. So Jake kept his eyes focused on his own business and turned up the volume on his earbuds to drown out the sound of his neighbors up high on their ladders, hammering and bitching under their breath about the goddamn storm. In short order, he became so focused on his task that he didn't hear the voice calling to him from the lawn next door, and when a hand tapped him on the shoulder from behind, he turned quickly to find the last person he expected to see on his lawn.

Christian Worthing was dressed in Khaki shorts with baggy cargo pockets, a dark blue T-shirt that clung to his upper body, accentuating his chest and shoulders, and leather sandals. With his short blond hair moussed in perfect disarray and his steely blue eyes fixed with guarded sincerity, he looked more like a teenage surfer than a twenty-seven-year-old stockbroker.

Christian smiled apologetically and said, "I didn't mean to spook you. I called from over there, but you were . . . "

He tapped his ear, and Jake removed his earbuds.

"Must be some pretty good jams," Christian said, and then he smiled again. "Or pretty loud. Maybe both."

His smile was tentative, but at least it was warmer than the stony glance Jake was used to receiving on days when they both happened to be outside at the same time, mowing their lawns or taking out the trash on Monday nights. Still, there was something about the smile that made Jake feel unsure, as if maybe he preferred the old arrangement where the two of them stayed on their own sides of the fence.

As if sensing Jake's thoughts, Christian glanced down at the shattered fence on the grass and said, "Maybe it's a sign, eh?" He smiled again, a less tentative smile. "Sometimes, He has to hit us over the head to get His message through. At least that's what my wife and Pastor Dan keep telling me."

Jake didn't quite know how to respond. He certainly didn't believe that the destruction of their neighborhood was the work of a mythical deity bent on bringing together two guys who shared nothing in common save for the white picket fence that divided their properties. So he remained respectfully silent.

Christian was still looking at the ruined fence when he said something unexpected. "My wife's been pushing me to come over and talk to you for a while. She thinks neighbors shouldn't be strangers." He looked up from the fallen fence and into Jake's eyes. "She told me how you helped her out last winter . . . when she backed into that snowbank and couldn't get her car out." He paused and took a breath. "That was upstanding, and I should have come over and thanked you. I really appreciate it."

He held his hand out, and after a moment, Jake took it. Christian's grip was firm, but not the bone-crushing vice grip Jake had half-expected, and his eyes looked sincere. Regardless, Jake was relieved when they both broke the handshake at the same time.

They stood there for a moment that might have become awkward. But then Christian said, "She went to Iowa, my wife, to stay with her parents. I didn't want her to be here when the storm hit—not with the baby on the way, you know? She's only three months along, but I didn't want to take any chances." He looked around the lawn. "And now I'm glad I didn't, you know?"

Jake nodded. "Better to be on the safe side."

With another look around the lawn, Christian released a sigh. "This is some mess, eh?"

Surveying the damage and downed power lines, Jake could not disagree with the assessment.

"You've lived here for a while, right? I mean, long enough to have seen one of these storms, right?"

Jake nodded again. He had seen a couple of storms in the Haven, though not quite as bad as this one.

"How long before the power gets restored?"

Jake shook his head. "It depends. A few days, usually. The longest was about four years ago. It was out for a week."

Christian looked shocked. "A week! You're kidding, right?"

Jake shook his head again. Christian laced his fingers together at the back of his neck and leaned back, releasing a sigh toward the sky. Jake couldn't help noticing the twin swells of Christian's bare upper arms.

"Well," Christian said, letting his arms fall back to his sides, "we lived without power for a couple thousand years before the light bulb came along, so I don't suppose a few days to a week will be all that bad."

It never failed to amaze Jake that an intelligent adult living in the twenty-first century could still believe that the world was only two thousand years old. Back in New York, he and his friends used to laugh off guys like Christian Worthing. But Dante's Haven wasn't New York. Here in this idyllic little hamlet, guys like Jake Leary were the odd men out—a fact that Jake was ever mindful of. In the neighboring city of Redemption, things were different. There, you could find just about every type of lifestyle, ethnicity, and persuasion, all coexisting openly and peacefully.

And it was there, at a sidewalk table outside of The Checkered Skirt, Redemption's premier gay bar, that Jake would find himself sharing that beer and chatting with his straitlaced neighbor less than eight hours after their first handshake.

three

They had agreed that the cleanup of their adjoining properties would go faster and more effectively if they worked together, and by midday, both of their front lawns were clear of all debris.

The back lawns had taken the brunt of the storm's abuse, and it took most of the rest of the day just to clear a quarter of the mess away. Under the baking sun, Jake had been tempted to peel off his shirt, but Christian had already removed his, and for some reason, Jake felt that following suit would send the wrong signal, that Christian would think Jake had perceived the removal of *his* shirt as an invitation for Jake to do the same. Jake had known a few guys in college who were dedicated "straight boy chasers," and they thrilled to the challenge of "turning" a straight boy for one memorable night of exploration and experimentation—especially a straight boy like Christian Worthing.

But pursuing straight boys for one-nighters wasn't Jake's thing. Indeed, right now he wasn't looking for *any* type of hookup. He had ended his three-year-long relationship with Marc a few months back, and the only thing he wanted now was some time alone. Not to reflect on what had gone wrong between Marc and him, because nothing had gone wrong. It had worked until it didn't, and the breakup had been both mutual and amicable.

He just needed time to reflect on himself and his priorities and figure out what he wanted from life. He had a rewarding career and enough money to live comfortably, and now he just needed to spend some time alone to figure out the rest—whatever "the rest" meant. But one thing he was sure of was that he had no interest in "turning" his straight neighbor for a night of drunken passion that, even if successful, would only lead to more cold glances from him across their property line.

As these thoughts passed through his mind like airy wisps of smoke down a distant tunnel, Jake stopped stacking the twisted aluminum panels and lifted his T-shirt to wipe the sweat from his brow. It was an unconscious gesture, and so he was taken by surprise when Christian said, "*Somebody's* shredded."

Christian had just come back from depositing a stack of rubbish at the side of the garage. He dropped a friendly wink and smile. Jake returned the smile, but looked confused. When Christian tipped a nod at Jake's rippled midsection, Jake flushed with embarrassment and dropped the hem of his T-shirt.

Christian shook his head with a wistful smile. "Don't tell me. You were a swimmer in high school—anchor in the 400m relay. Probably on the soccer team, too—attacking midfielder—am I right?"

Jake nodded, with a curious half-smile, wondering how Christian had pegged both spot-on.

Christian chuckled. "I'll bet you don't even have to work at it, do you?" He shook his head again and sighed. "It comes so easy for you lean guys. I had a buddy back in Iowa—James Minkus—tall, lean, toned guy, just like you. He had the tightest rack of abs, I swear to shit, and it just came so effortlessly for him." He laughed with a twinkle of nostalgia in his eyes. "We used to work out together in his basement—it smelled like dank ass, but it was cool." On Jake's quizzical look, Christian laughed again and said, "You had to grow up on an Iowa farm to understand it. Anyway, James used to bitch all the time about how he wished he could get bigger and gain muscle mass like me— the guy was in love with my chest and shoulders; he called me Superman."

They both laughed over that one, but Jake was surprised on two counts. The first was at Christian's use of language; he hadn't expected the guy Marc had dubbed "Captain America" to use words like "shit" and "ass"—at least not with such casual alacrity. The second was at his new perception of "Captain America"—despite their differences, Jake Leary found himself warming up to Christian Worthing.

"But you know what the shit of it is?" Christian went on while stroking his bare chest absently. "I'd have traded builds with him in a New York minute. It takes a ton of work to keep this body in this shape. If I stopped, I'd become a lard-ass in less than six months. Believe me, I've seen tons of my friends go to shit after college, eating pizza for dinner every night and drinking like it's going out of style—*I'd* like to eat pizza every night, but not at that cost."

He laughed and shook his head again. Jake remained silent but intrigued.

"I've put way too much work into this," Christian said, with an unconscious glance down at his flexed forearms. "It's the temple, after all." He looked at Jake and smiled. "I'm not like a total narcissist or anything like that. I just like to stay in shape, you know."

It wasn't a question, but Jake nodded anyway.

Christian said, "I went to my ten-year high school reunion last month, and Minkus was there, still as tall and lean and carved as ever, and they served this deep dish pizza, and that son of a bitch ate like four slices, can you believe that? Unreal!" He chuckled—an infectious sound that made Jake smile again—and then his eyes narrowed and still chuckling, he said, "You're like that, aren't you. You can load up on junk and not gain an ounce of fat, you svelte bitch. I'm right, aren't I."

Again, it wasn't a question, and again Jake nodded. Only this time, his smile was a bit sly. And then suddenly they were both laughing again—the sort of laughter that comes seemingly out of nowhere between close friends who have known each other for years, not complete strangers who've only just met.

Christian was still laughing as he picked up another stack of debris and headed back to the garage. On his way, he called back, "Don't be a pussy, bro. It's fuckin' hot out here. Take off your shirt and let that body you were blessed with breathe."

Jake stood in the baking afternoon sunlight, his gaze locked on the glistening bronzed back of his next-door neighbor as the guy headed toward the garage.

For a second, Jake could have almost sworn he heard something at the back of his mind, like a bell. Or an alarm.

But then, as quickly as it came, it faded, and with his eyes still locked on Christian Worthing's bare back and broad shoulders (the sort that he himself had never been able to achieve, no matter how hard he worked out), Jake Leary peeled off his T-shirt and pitched it aside.

four

It was nearly dusk by the time they'd gone into their separate houses to wash up after the day's work. With the power still out all over the Haven, Christian suggested they hit one of the eateries in the neighboring village of Redemption, and Jake agreed.

They had pasta at the Italian restaurant where Christian and his wife had celebrated their first wedding anniversary back in April. Jake was surprised when, after their meal, Christian suggested they stop for a drink (Christian only had water at dinner, so Jake had assumed he wasn't a drinker). Jake had no intention of going to The Checkered Skirt—he figured that Christian would want to go to the sports bar at the opposite end of Redemption Boulevard, and so he was doubly surprised when on their way down the block Christian tipped a nod at The Skirt and said, "How 'bout there?" On Jake's dubious look, Christian raised a brow. "What? You don't think I can handle a drink at a gay bar?"

"Nah, I just assumed . . . "

Christian smiled. "I know a few Log Cabin Republicans. I'm not a judgmental guy."

Jake shook his head with a smile of his own, "It's cool. Just don't expect to see any of them in there."

The place was so crowded that they ended up sitting at one of the sidewalk tables, which turned out to be a nice spot. Though the temperature was in the low eighties and the humidity was still high, a pleasant breeze passed along the cobblestone sidewalk.

They'd polished off their first beers and were making progress on the second round when Christian, looking more comfortable outside of a gay bar than Jake would have expected, said, "You know we're going to have to come back here so I can prove to you that I'm not afraid to go inside, right?"

He was smiling a little slyly, like maybe he wanted Jake to believe that he was a little buzzed. Jake doubted that a guy in Christian's shape could get buzzed on less than two beers, especially not on a full stomach of pasta and bread-sticks. Still, his curiosity was piqued, and he returned Christian's smile.

Christian laughed, a genuine laugh that peaked in a short, high-pitched sound before trailing off into a sigh. He took another sip of his beer and said, "I know what you're thinking. You don't think I know it, but I know what you're thinking,"

"What am I thinking?" Jake inquired gamely.

"You're thinking—and I don't blame you for it—you're thinking that I'm just dickin' with you—"

Jake shook his head to indicate that he did not think Christian was dicking with him, but Christian wasn't fin-ished.

"It's OK, man. I know what you see in me, and that's cool. I know I give off the 'vibe'—"

Jake raised an eyebrow. "The 'vibe?'"

Christian laughed. "You know the vibe I'm talking about. The 'hardass straight guy vibe.' But honestly, I'm not that kind of straight guy. I have no problem with alternative lifestyles. I wouldn't be sitting here with you if I did. I'm cool with it. I'm not gonna try to lure you into my church for conversion therapy or anything like that—I don't even believe in that crap. You are what you are, just like I am what I am, and nothing can change that. And nothing should. Like I said, I have Log Cabin friends at work. I'm not the kind of guy who freaks out if some guy checks out my ass." He took another healthy sip of his beer and smiled. "In fact, I take it as a compliment."

Jake studied Christian for a moment. "Are you asking me if I think you have a nice ass?"

"Nah, man," Christian said, laughing. "I mean, yeah, if you think I do, you could say it, and I wouldn't be a dick about it. I mean, like, I *have* an ego—anybody who looks like me has an ego, and if they tell you they don't, they're lying. But I'm just saying I don't care if a guy checks me out. I'm secure enough in my sexuality. I know who I am. I may not be into guys, but it's still a boost to my ego when I catch one of them checking me out, you know?"

The naked sincerity in Christian's eyes struck a chord in Jake, and he couldn't help thinking of all the nameless, faceless guys who'd stolen glances at Christian Worthing over the years—at schools, parks, malls, in locker rooms after gym class. He couldn't help thinking of the desire they'd harbored yet dared not speak of.

For his own part, Jake could not deny that Christian Worthing was, as his ex, Marc, had once put it without hyperbole, a "breathtaking show-stopper." And he could see how easily Christian must have factored into the fantasies of countless guys who'd merely come into casual contact with him. And he could only imagine what any one of those guys would give to trade places with him right now. What would they give to be sitting here on this warm night outside of The Checkered Skirt with Christian Worthing? To gaze into those sincere blue eyes and be the sole subject of their focus, to hear him say it was OK for them to check him out, that he liked it when their eyes lingered on him—what sacrifice would they be willing to make for that?

Christian suddenly acquired a sheepish grin and shook his head. "I probably shouldn't tell you this—I've never told anyone this—not even my wife, I swear it—but back in college . . . "

Christian trailed off, and his cheeks flushed. Jake felt the urge to prompt him, but suppressed it. And momentarily, his patience paid off.

Christian chuckled and, with his cheeks still burning, said, "Back in college, I took a part-time job at a strip club—God, I can't believe I'm telling you this. It wasn't like a total nude thing, my junk was always covered, in a G-string, you know?" He shook his head again. Only this time, he seemed more amused than embarrassed. "I was young at the time—nineteen—and it was at this ladies' club, and I needed the money. It was OK, and I only did it on weekends, just for extra cash. But then this guy I worked with got hired at this other place, and he told me he could get me in."

Christian took another sip of his beer. Jake waited silently, but his heart was beating with anticipation, even though he was pretty sure what was coming next.

"Turned out it was a gay club," Christian said with a small smile. "At first, I was a little freaked out. I mean, stripping for a crowd of chicks was one thing, but I wasn't sure I could do something like that in front of guys, you know? I mean, no offense, but that's just not my thing.

"Anyway, I'll never forget my first night. My heart was beating like crazy. It was so bad I thought I was going to have a heart attack or something. I mean, it was beating like crazy fast. I was standing backstage, dressed in this tear-away costume. It was a Navy costume—not a squid uniform but an officer's dress whites, you know? And my fuckin' heart is pounding so loud I can't hear anything that's going on around me. All I can hear is my heart drumming and the crowd cheering for the guy who went out before me. I'm telling you, I was so scared—I've never been that scared in my entire life—I couldn't think straight."

He paused, and his eyes looked haunted for a moment. Then he picked up the thread of the story with vigor.

"And then somebody gave me a nudge from behind and said, 'You're up, dude.' But it wasn't until I was out there on the stage—it was one of those circular stages with the ramp leading onto it, you know? But it wasn't until I was out there, under those lights, hearing that crowd, that I realized what it was that scared me. And it wasn't the stripping part of it at all. It was the reaction of the crowd. Not that they'd get too excited and rush the stage or something, but that they wouldn't get excited at all. I was terrified that they'd just sit there in dead silence until one of them started laughing. And I was positive that once that happened, they'd all join in because they'd know I was a fraud, and they'd just laugh me off the stage."

Christian uttered a short chuckle, and his eyes shone with a hint of nostalgia. Jake looked at him in silence.

"But they didn't laugh," Christian said. "They cheered. And when I ripped off the costume, they went wild. I mean, you've never heard anything like this—or at least *I* never had. It wasn't like being on drugs, but like a *natural* high, like you could die right there because nothing could ever feel more . . . uplifting than that, you know?"

This time, Jake did speak. "You got bit by the bug."

Christian looked confused.

"The showbiz bug," Jake elaborated. "Being onstage."

Christian nodded. "Yeah, I guess. But it was more than just that. It was the cheering and applause and whistling. It was like . . . " He trailed off with that distant look of nostalgia in his eyes once again and then came back to himself. "It was like the guys were more appreciative than the girls, you know? And somehow more respectful. I mean, yeah, some of them reached up for a pat or a touch, and I didn't mind it. But the women . . . they'd actually grab you, try to yank you off the stage. Not all of them, but some of them, and it felt more aggressive, you know? But the gay guys were more like . . . gentleman about it, you know? Like I said, they'd touch, but they didn't grab and try to pull you off the stage. And after the show, like girls would be all over you, trying to get a date and shit. And some of the guys would do that too, but it's like they were cool with it when you told them you weren't interested in hooking up. With the gay guys, you didn't have to worry about one of them showing up outside the window of your dorm room, drunk off his ass in the middle of the night and waking up the whole campus blasting love songs from a boombox, you know? That actually happened with this one crazy chick, I swear it!"

Christian shook his head and sighed. Jake gave a scarcely perceptible nod.

"And the *tips*," Christian went on, with that nostalgic look in his eyes again, "the tips were un-fuckin'-believable! I don't care what anyone says, gay guys are definitely *not* stingy pricks when it comes to tipping."

Christian raised his glass with a grin and polished off the rest in a single swallow. Then he looked at Jake, rolled his eyes, and let out that high-pitched laugh of his again. "We're gonna *have* to get drunk now, so I can forget that I ever told you that boring story. I'm sorry, man."

But he didn't look sorry. He looked happy and loose and carefree. When the server brought another two drafts, he gave him a twenty and told him to keep the change. Then, he raised his glass to Jake and said, "See? I can be like you guys."

Jake laughed, a genuine laugh this time.

Christian sipped his beer with a grin and said, "You know what I mean. Now shut the fuck up and get drunk with me."

five

They had a few more rounds, but they didn't get drunk. The night ended on a positive note, with the two of them shaking hands in Christian's driveway and heading into their separate houses to get some much-needed rest.

Jake didn't lie awake half the night pondering Christian's revelation about being a stripper at a gay club back in his college days. Indeed, he drifted off to sleep within moments of his head hitting the pillow, and if he had any dreams, he didn't remember them. Thoughts of his night out with his not-so-straitlaced next-door neighbor only came the following morning when he woke to the bright sunlight pouring through his bedroom window.

At first, it felt like the entire previous day had been one long dream. But as he got dressed for the next phase of the cleanup duties that awaited him on the lawn and the lake outside, the reality of the night before began to creep in. And with it came the feeling that he would not be greeted by the same happy-go-lucky guy that he'd shared several pints of beer with the night before.

It was the story that Christian had told him; Jake was positive of that. Maybe the guy actually *was* capable of getting buzzed on only a couple of beers—buzzed enough to let out a secret that, by the light of day, he would regret sharing. Or maybe Christian had just gotten worked up by being at a gay bar and wanted to prove what a tolerant guy he was to his gay next-door neighbor. Either way, by the time Jake had finished his breakfast of oatmeal and toast, he had managed to convince himself of one thing: Christian Worthing would not be greeting him with a friendly smile, raring to get started on their joint venture of cleaning up the mess left by the storm.

His prediction appeared to be confirmed when he stepped outside and saw no change to the condition of the adjacent lawns and no sign of Christian. He was surprised at the sinking sensation within him. It wasn't like he'd expected that Christian and he would suddenly become best buddies. But he couldn't deny that he'd enjoyed having someone to work with on the cleanup, and further, that he'd enjoyed Christian's company.

With one last look at the expanse of his lawn and a silent sigh of resignation, Jake stepped down from the wide porch and headed out to commence the day's work on his own.

It was shortly after 7:00 A.M. when Jake heard a horn honking, and Christian's maroon Grand Cherokee pulled into his driveway. Through the windshield, Jake saw Christian throw up his arms and make a "what gives?" expression. When Jake looked at him quizzically, Christian broke into a broad grin and stepped out of the vehicle with a white box with orange and pink print on it in one hand

and a cardboard drink carrier with two cups of coffee in the other.

"I left like super early," he called out, "so I could get back before you got up, but the line was like ten miles long!"

Jake approached, and Christian set the coffee carrier on the Jeep's hood and opened the box.

"I didn't know what kind you liked, so I got one of everything. And don't even *try* to tell me that you don't eat doughnuts, bitch, because America runs on Dunkin'."

They ate the doughnuts straight out of the box on the hood of Christian's Jeep while surveying the lawns. They didn't discuss a plan of attack; they just set about the task in the same fashion as they'd done the previous day. The only difference was that this time they had a dumpster to dispose of the refuse (Christian had taken the liberty of calling the number on the side of the unit down the street, and a mid-sized unit was delivered to his driveway by noon).

They worked until six-thirty and then broke for a dinner of takeout pizza and Cokes. Jake thought they would be calling it a night when they headed into their separate dwellings to shower off the day's sweat and grime. He was actually looking forward to getting some extra sleep before resuming cleanup duty the following morning. But it didn't turn out that way.

When he stepped from the shower, a text was waiting on his phone. It was from Christian. It read: YOU UP FOR A COUPLE OF COLD ONES? I'M BUYING.

Jake looked at his bed through the open doorway across the hall with a longing expression. He was tired, but a beer sounded good, so he responded to the text with: SURE.

He began to towel off when a second message came

through: THE CHECKERED SKIRT? I STILL HAVE TO PROVE THAT I'M
NOT AFRAID TO GO INSIDE. ;-)

Jake couldn't help smiling at that one. And by the time
he was dressed and downstairs, he didn't feel so tired
anymore. He felt refreshed and ready to brave the inside
of Redemption's premiere gay bar with his new straitlaced
friend. That's what they were, he supposed: friends. Or at
least friendly neighbors.

But they didn't end up inside the bar. Not because
Christian wasn't willing—he was actually eager to prove
that he wasn't afraid to step up to the challenge—but
because of an unexpected turn of events that neither of
them could have foreseen.

six

They pulled up to The Checkered Skirt shortly after eight in Jake's BMW i4. Jake had thought Christian would want to drive, as he'd done the night before. But when they met outside, Christian didn't go to his Jeep. Instead, he headed straight for Jake's driveway and quipped with a grin, "Let's see how much kick this little battery buggy of yours has, brother."

By the time they arrived at their destination, Christian's grin was no longer derisive.

"Pretty smooth, teach," he said with a respectful nod. "Got some serious torque. I thought it'd be more like a golf cart." He gave a short laugh that ended with his standard high-pitched squeal. "At least it's not one of those mini rice-burners you Lefties love. This thing's got some serious muscle under the hood." He dropped Jake a wink and a grin, like they were in on a secret. "It's sleek and silent . . . sort of like you. Sweet ride."

Jake returned the smile but without the wink. He knew that Christian didn't mean anything personal by the "you

Lefties" comment. But he also thought the reason Christian had wanted him to drive was that Christian didn't want any of the patrons of The Checkered Skirt to see the MAGA bumper sticker on his Jeep.

Nymphomania's *I Want Your Body* greeted them as they headed up the sidewalk. It was blaring at full volume from the sound system inside The Skirt, and Jake couldn't help noticing the fine hair rising on Christian's forearms in response to the pulsating techno beat.

They were stopped at the entrance by a young guy in jeans and a black T-shirt that clung to his chiseled upper body like a second skin. The discreet logo on the T-shirt's pocket was a checkered skirt upended to look like a martini glass with an olive skewered by a toothpick. He told them The Skirt was at capacity, but they could still have drinks at one of the outdoor tables. Christian looked over the doorman's shoulders and through the glass entrance. The place was packed, and for a second, Jake thought Christian was going to try to smooth-talk the guy into letting them in, but instead, Christian just smiled and nodded like it was all good.

The doorman said it was "dance fever night" and that the crowd would thin out in an hour when the Flamingo turned on its cosmic lights. The Flamingo was the mini golf course up the street that nobody went to until after sundown . . . and with enough drinks in them to enjoy the neon-lit fairways. Christian smiled like he could dig it and introduced himself as "Saxon."

"And this is my little brother, Lochlan," he added with a nod toward Jake. He grinned at Jake's reaction to the lie and said in a confidential tone to the doorman, "He's shy."

The doorman introduced himself as Keanu (which

was actually his real name; it was stitched in flowing script below the logo on his form-fitting T-shirt), and he and Christian exchanged a handshake in a complex and smoothly executed series of gestures, like frat brothers at a kegger.

"Can we get a couple of brews, man?"

Keanu said, "Any particular preference?"

"Nothing domestic," Christian said with a grin. "It's Lochy's twenty-first today, and I want to bust his cherry properly."

Keanu grinned like he could dig it and winked at Jake, who smiled bashfully, which made him look precisely as Christian had presented him: a twenty-one-year-old out for his first drink with his big brother.

"How do you do that?" Jake asked after they'd settled into their seats opposite each other at a table in the gated patio dining area.

"Do what?" Christian asked with the hint of a sincere smile.

"Make it up on the fly like that?"

Christian shrugged.

"Do you think he bought it?" Jake asked.

Christian crinkled his eyes as if to say, "Bought what?"

"That you and I are brothers," Jake said, "and that you're taking me out for my first beer."

Christian laughed. "God, no! Look at us! You look more like *him* than me, with your dark hair and dreamy hazel eyes. He thinks we're *frat* brothers. But he totally buys that you're twenty-one. You can't be much older than that anyway."

"I'm twenty-six."

Christian shrugged again. "I'm twenty-seven. It's just

numbers. But we *look* younger. Especially you. I'm surprised Keanu didn't card your ass." He laughed again.

Jake wasn't surprised when Keanu brought the drinks himself—he suspected that Keanu was interested in Christian. But he was surprised when Keanu set a basket of mozzarella sticks on the table with the bottles of beer. "On the house. For the birthday boy," he added with a smile at Jake.

"Aren't you going to card me?" Jake didn't know why he asked this question—he was usually more reserved with strangers.

Keanu just grinned and said, "Now why would I do that?" And with a wink at Christian, he asked, "You vouch for him?"

Christian nodded, "He's legal." And with a grin, he added, "Just barely."

Keanu laughed. He had perfect teeth. "Let me know when you're ready for another round."

They drank their beers while chatting about tomorrow's cleanup. Christian said they should probably check the roofs for missing and damaged tiles. Jake said he would call a roofer in the morning, and Christian scoffed with a smile, "Fuck that. We don't need a bean crew up there, tearing out flashing and pitching it over the side, ruining the lawn." Perhaps noticing the slight flicker in Jake's eyes, he added, "We don't need any white-trash retards, drunk off their pampered college asses, either. It's just a couple of loose shingles, most likely. We can do it ourselves." He tagged Jake on the arm with a grin. "The two musketeers. I'm Aramis, God's blade of justice. You're Athos, Comte de la Fère—secretive but trustworthy, and good in a fight."

Jake gave a curious smile. Christian laughed and

raised a brow as he took a bite out of a mozzarella stick and washed it down with a swig of beer.

"What? You didn't think a dumb Iowa farm boy like me would know the classics? I've read them all, and some that most people never even heard of—*The Black Tulip, Captain Pamphile, Amaury, The Wolf Leader,* which is the first story ever about a werewolf, and *The Pale Lady,* one of the earliest recorded vampire stories. Do you know it?"

Jake nodded; he did know it. *The Pale Lady* was included in Dumas's *The Thousand and One Ghosts,* though it wasn't really a ghost story. It told the tale of a beautiful young Polish noblewoman who is sent to a monastery in the Carpathian Mountains for protection against the invading Russian forces. Once ensconced there, she meets two very different brothers who fall in love with her. As Jake recalled, the tale ended tragically.

"And, of course," Christian said, biting into another mozzarella stick, "I've read all of the Musketeer books— the original, *Twenty Years After,* and *The Vicomte de Bragelonne*— about a thousand times each." He shot a guilty smile across the table and said, "These are fuckin' awesome. You'd better catch up before I wolf them all."

Jake took a mozzarella stick and bit into it. They ate in silence until Jake noticed that Christian was looking at him with an oddly serene expression.

"What?" Jake said, feeling a bit self-conscious.

Christian shook his head. "Nothing. It's just the way you chew. You take your time, nice and slow, like a deer in the woods. And you don't drink in between bites, like most people. You always wait until you're done chewing."

Jake's chewing slowed even more, and he half-smiled, not sure if this was a compliment or a criticism. He finished chewing, picked up his bottle, and tipped the stem to his lips.

It was too late for Jake to stop the flow of beer going down his throat when Christian grinned and commanded softly, "Now, swallow."

To his credit, Jake managed to get the drink down without spraying beer across the table. But he laughed and coughed, sending a spray out of his nostrils and onto his shirt. This sent Christian into gales of laughter, like a teen-ager at a campfire.

"Oh my God, dude, you should see your face!" Christian cried with laughter.

Jake wiped the beer from his chin and shirt, muttering, "You're a dick." But he was smiling when he said it, and this only made Christian laugh harder.

When Keanu returned and asked if they were ready for another round, Christian pulled out his wallet and laid a couple of bills on the table. "Yeah, and a bib and a nipple for my baby brother's bottle if you've got it. He's still not house-trained."

Keanu smiled and picked up the bills. "I'll bring him a bar towel."

"Thanks, man. Sorry about the mess." When Keanu was gone, Christian turned to Jake with a not-entirely-guilty smile. "I'm sorry, dude. I couldn't resist. You just look so serious all the time."

Jake shook his head, like it was all good. And when he smiled a small smile and said, "Payback'll be a bitch," Christian rolled into fresh gales of laughter.

Keanu returned with two beers, a bar towel, and a small bottle of club soda. When he tried to give Christian his change from the beers, Christian waved it off and said,

"Keep it, man. I'm sure this one's got a few more messes in him."

After Keanu was gone, Jake looked up while dabbing his shirt with the club soda and said, "Twelve bucks. That's a pretty good tip."

"He's cool," Christian said, taking a swig from his fresh beer. "He can be our Porthos."

"Isn't that the fat one?"

Christian shook his head. "Common misconception, created by the Hollywood elites. In the books, Porthos is strong and virile. Depardieu should be ashamed of himself for playing Porthos as a bumbling, fat drunk in that movie. Malkovich, Irons, and Byrne were awesome. Even that whiny little bitch, Libtardo DiCaprio, was decent as the twin kings. But Depardieu turning Porthos into a fart joke was a complete desecration."

Jake was struck by Christian's vehemence over the bad casting of a simple movie adaptation, but not surprised. It was his favorite author, and Jake supposed the guy had the right to be a little pissed about it.

Almost as if he'd read Jake's thoughts, Christian said, "It's not the casting, or Depardieu—he could've played it perfectly if they'd written the character like he was in the books. How hard can it be to write it when you've got the book right there in front of you?"

Jake nodded understandingly.

Christian sighed, taking another sip of his beer. He looked off, toward the entrance where Keanu was still redirecting patrons to the patio seats. "Nah," he said with a smile at Jake. "Keanu over there is our Porthos."

Jake nodded and sipped his beer. "Good choice."

Christian's smile became a smooth grin. "Now all we

need is our D'Artagnan." He raised a brow and added, "Of course, he'll have to be really pretty—we can't have Athos being prettier than D'Artagnan, and let's face it, *you're* a real pretty boy, teach. Hell, a couple more beers, and *I'll* be trying to get up your skirt!"

This made Jake flush and smile with embarrassment, and, in turn, his embarrassment made Christian laugh. And pretty soon, they were both laughing.

seven

They remained on the patio even after the "dance fever" crowd had cleared out of the bar and headed for the neon lights of the cosmic mini golf course up the street. When Keanu came to their table to let them know that the bar and dance floor were open again, Christian just shook his head politely and said they'd stay put. Raising a brow in Jake's direction, he added, "If that's cool with you, Lochy. I mean, there's no point in dancing if there's nobody left to dance with, right?"

From his patio seat, Jake had a good view through the bar's front window, and there were still quite a few guys on the dance floor, but he nodded in agreement with Christian and ordered another round.

Keanu returned shortly with two bottles of beer and a complimentary tray of nachos (Christian's generous tips had continued to flow, and Jake suspected that Keanu felt obligated to pay a little back).

They were sipping their beers and discussing the best of *The Three Musketeers* film adaptations. Christian's favorite was the 2011 version—though he thought Logan Lerman's D'Artagnan stood out like a sore thumb, the rest of the cast was spot on, particularly the Musketeers, and especially Ray Stevenson, who "nailed the role of Porthos."

"I can't believe he's gone," Christian said, shaking his head sadly. "Awesome actor. God must have needed him in His troop of thespians."

For a second, Jake expected Christian to break into another grin and wink at him. But there was no sign of a joke in Christian's eyes. He was serious.

Something must have flickered in Jake's eyes because Christian smiled and said, "I take it you're not very religious. It's cool. I'm not looking to convert you. 'Live and let live' is my motto."

It was quiet for a moment, and Jake felt the need to respond. "No, I'm cool with that. I'm just not sure of the whole church thing."

"Neither am I," said Christian. He took another sip of his beer. "I don't need a church telling me what I already know in my heart. I've got Jesus right here." He tapped his chest, and his nostrils flared briefly.

"You really believe that." It wasn't a question, and Jake wasn't playing coy.

"Absolutely," Christian said. "Jesus is my boy. Been there by my side my entire life. And he's gonna be there for the whole nine—plus extra innings if I'm blessed enough to play them—until God calls me home."

If Jake had heard this from anyone else, he would have laughed. But coming from Christian, it didn't sound laughable at all. He was trying to think of a way to respond when the aleatoric hand of fate intervened.

Christian saw the attractive young woman approaching

from the sidewalk outside of the gated dining area before Jake noticed anything more than her perfume—a woody aromatic fragrance with notes of bergamot, vetiver, and lavender: "gypsy water," his mother's older sister, Becky, had called it. At first, Christian thought the young woman was panhandling for change and automatically reached for his pocket. But the woman spoke to Jake—and she wasn't looking for loose pocket change.

"Are you looking to be husband?"

Her question was so direct and put so matter-of-factly that Christian's jaw dropped, and he uttered a short laugh of disbelief.

Jake could hardly credit what he'd heard either and said, "Excuse me?"

The girl had a thick accent, and it was possible that Christian and Jake had simply misunderstood her. When she repeated the question, Jake froze and then smiled tenuously, looking around, sure that he would spot someone close by with a camera. This had to be a joke, like on one of those TV shows—*Punk'd* or *The Jamie Kennedy Experiment*. It simply couldn't be real. With flushed cheeks, Jake said, "I'm sorry. Do I know you?"

"Probably not," the young woman said, waving off the question. "But you are looking to be husband." Her eyes shifted between Jake and Christian, expectantly. "Good husband. Faithful. Right?"

Jake looked at Christian, who laughed that short, incredulous laugh again. If Christian had set this up as a joke, he was doing a phenomenal job of acting just as bemused as Jake was by the whole thing.

Before Jake could respond, the girl said, "I'm not ask for self. I'm ask for friend, who is just come over from Ukraine."

She pointed to the car behind her, where a young guy sat in the passenger seat, his face half-cast in shadow. Only his eyes were visible. They were a stunning hazel, shot with greenish-blue streaks that seemed to shimmer under the dim glow of a nearby street lamp. Jake assumed it could have just been a trick of the light, but the left eye appeared to be slightly darker than the right.

"He is gypsy from Ukraine, like me," she said, "but will be born in 'Merica, so to be 'Merican. Also Chechen because one father Chechen, and other 'Merican. But mother is Ukrainian gypsy and smart like 'Merican, so move him here before is conceive. She is die since move him—killed by the fascist pig, Putin. You know the pig Putin? Is friends with the orange clown. Very bad man, kill lots of Ukraine. But her spirit live on in boy, who escape to live safe, happy life and grow strong in 'Merica. Handsome boy, very handsome. You see?"

Jake could see the young man was indeed handsome—strikingly handsome, in fact. Further, he understood that the young woman was not referring to the Romani people when she used the term "gypsy." She was using it to describe herself and the boy as wanderers, outcasts searching for a place in a world that scarcely knew they existed, or cared.

"But now that 'Merica is run by fascists, boy will be taken by ICE—you know ICE? They will take him back to Ukraine to be killed, or worse, to become slave of the pig Putin."

Jake looked at the boy sitting quietly in the passenger seat. He wasn't alone. A cat sat up on his lap, with ears perked up and eyes looking about the night. He was a sinewy feline of average stature with bright eyes and a long tail that stood up proud and straight. His fur was short, sleek, and patchy. His muzzle was white, save for a black-spotted beige patch on the right side and a fleck of dark beige on the left close to his nose.

"His name is Dzhokhar—the boy, not the kotchka—but nobody likes that name because it sounds like 'Joker,' the crazy man with the white face and the red mouth and the green hair who causes all the trouble for the Batman. You know the Batman? So we just call him 'Nacho' because he likes nachos, and he looks like Ignacio. You know Ignacio? The model on the big boards in the underwear—the one with the beautiful skin and the dark eyes and the messy hair? Very handsome. Ignacio is Ignacio Cordova, but they call him 'Nacho,' and he looks like Dzhokhar, so we just call Dzhokhar 'Nacho,' too. He's in car over there. See? Very handsome. Very fit. Healthy teeth. Looking for nice 'Merican make family. Good boy. Strong, too. Not like your friend here with the big muscles." She nodded at Christian. "More like you. Lean. But strong. Very obedient. You like him. He like you. Quiet boy, like you. Want to meet?"

Jake was taken aback by the rapid-fire barrage of information and said the first thing that came to mind. "What does he do?"

"Anything you want. Very obedient."

"No. What does he do for a living? A job."

"No job. But work hard. Very strong. Nice muscles. Looks like model. Strong like Iron Man. Good boy, make family with you. Come for green card, stay for love. Very affectionate. Very loyal. Clean. You are Jew, no?"

Jake's eyes crinkled curiously, and his lips parted. But before he could speak, the girl went on.

"You are Ashkenazi; boy is same. No foreskin. Very

clean. Good hygiene. Handsome, like you. Mother is die young. Like you, left with father to raise. Very smart. Teach self to read and write, like you. Words just make sense to him at very young age, like you. Very smart boy." She shot a look of appraisal at Christian. "Strong like you—but not with the big muscles. But brave, and know the stick with the ball you play—a natural like you. Make you proud." Her eyes darted back to Jake. "You must trust the white wolf—is only one who can protect boy when kotchka is off running. Kotchka is like whore, runs by night, every night—always the pussy he is seeking. But loves boy, will defend with life like tiger!" Then her eyes shifted between Jake and Christian. "Good match. You make marry. Make good union. Both handsome. Good match. Long, happy life together. Boy do anything you want. Very obedient."

Jake shook his head. "I'm sorry. I don't speak Chechen."

"Neither does boy. He speaks with hands, like deaf."

"He's deaf?"

"No. *Speaks* like deaf. Is hearing like bell. Likes loud 'Merican music. Just doesn't speak. Except with hands, like deaf. You speak like deaf with hands, yes?"

Jake looked at her, but didn't say anything.

"Have seen you with deaf, speaking with hands, and think to self: Good match. Both handsome. Boy speak with hands like deaf, too. Good communication. Good understanding. Nothing lost in translation. Good match. You marry, keep boy. Two dads. Is all legal now, man to marry man, yes? Be happy. Live long, happy life."

Jake looked at the car again. The cat sat up now on the boy's lap with his front paws on the open window, gazing out expectantly with his heterochromatic eyes—one blue, one green.

The girl said, "Kotchka comes with boy. Package deal. Boy loves kotchka. Kotchka loves boy. Very devoted. Kotchka will die for boy—very protective, very fierce with claws to defend. Gentle as kitten with the purring if boy is safe. If boy threatened, then kotchka become crazy like tiger." She pronounce the word "tiger" as "*toiger*." She looked at Jake. "You good man. You no hurt boy. Kotchka know this. Kotchka purr like kitten for you. No worries."

Jake looked at the boy in the passenger seat of the convertible, wondering how old he could be. Seventeen? Eighteen?

As if reading Jake's thoughts, the girl said, "He will be nineteen when leaves fall. Just before leaves fall. Libra— love, balance, harmony. Make good family. Very faithful. Kotchka make good watchdog, too. Protect you and boy from fascists."

Jake shook his head in wonder and smiled sadly at the girl. "I'm sorry, I can't help you."

He'd half expected her to press the issue further, and was a bit surprised when she simply nodded and said "OK," and headed back to the car.

Jake met the boy's solemn gaze, and the boy smiled timidly at him, signing, "Nice to meet you," before the car pulled away from the curb.

After the taillights had faded into the night, Christian turned back to Jake with a crooked smile and chuckled disbelievingly, "What the hell was *that* all about?"

Jake didn't answer. He just shook his head as he continued to gaze into the darkness of the night, where the car with the girl, the boy, and the cat had seemed to vanish like the rabbit in a smoothly executed magic trick.

eight

Later that night, as he lay in bed, Jake thought of the strange meeting with the young woman on the patio outside of The Checkered Skirt. She was an attractive girl with the body of a track runner or a swimmer. He thought of her lovely green eyes and how they seemed at once both alight with fervent expectation and paradoxically demure. He thought of her creamy, unblemished skin, save for a smattering of freckles on her nose, which did not detract from her beauty. And again, he was struck by her direct, almost matter-of-fact manner as she offered up the boy to a complete stranger, as if she'd stepped straight from the pages of an old novel set in a bygone era where people were traded into marriage in exchange for parcels of land or livestock.

Very handsome. Very fit. Healthy teeth . . . Good boy. Strong, too . . . Very obedient.

But it was the other things she'd said that had really given Jake pause—the personal information that she had no way of knowing.

You are Ashkenazi; boy is same . . . Mother is die young. Like you, left with father to raise. Very smart. Teach self to read and write, like you. Words just make sense to him at very young age, like you. Very smart boy.

Jake didn't know if what she had said about Christian was also accurate, but it sounded pretty much on the money . . .

Strong like you—but not with the big muscles. But brave, and know the stick with the ball you play—a natural like you. Make you proud.

Possibly, she was just taking an educated stab—Christian was athletically built and easily could have been a natural at baseball. But how in the world could she have known that Jake was an Ashkenazi? Or that his mother had died young when he was still a kid? Or that he had taught himself to read and write?

Words just make sense to him at very young age, like you. Very smart boy.

Jake thought about the videos he'd seen on "psychics" in college psychology classes—the way they used things you told them about yourself to make you believe that they had genuine psychic abilities. But the girl hadn't given him or Christian the chance to speak. She'd just rolled straight into her spiel without interest beyond selling them on the idea of taking the kid.

And what was her endgame? What did she expect to get out of the arrangement? Money? Something else? And why had she given up so easily and headed back to the car without a fight?

None of it made sense.

Jake was still pondering the weird scene on the patio outside The Checkered Skirt when his eyelids began to feel heavy, and he drifted off to sleep as easily as he had done the previous evening . . . only this time, his sleep was not dreamless. He didn't toss and turn throughout the night, and he didn't dream about the woman or the Ashkenazi boy—at least not that he could remember.

He dreamt about Christian.

The dream came shortly before dawn, and it was a memorable one.

In this dream, he was standing in a field in Iowa, looking out across an endless stretch of waving wheat. He was barefoot and shirtless. His hair lifted and danced across his forehead in the autumn breeze as he gazed at the golden sunrise over the wheat. And he wasn't alone.

Christian stood beside him, barefoot and shirtless, too, his blue eyes fixed on the area below the sunrise. The wheat was rustling, like the tall grass in one of those Jurassic Park movies—the scene where the velociraptors were stalking their prey in straight lines from multiple directions.

But there was only one line here, and it was zigzagging right at them . . . with a long tail bobbing straight up behind, like a shark fin cutting through water.

Christian scoffed, "Those fucking voles are going to destroy the wheat before we can harvest it—the kotchka is after them." He pointed to the long, raised tail cutting a swath through the wheat like the tail of a raptor. "But he's not going to be able to do it on his own." With flared nostrils, Christian unzipped and stripped off his jeans. "Only one way to deal with this. Wish me luck, bro."

Christian cupped the back of Jake's neck with a warm hand and kissed him—not a passionate kiss, but there was a hint of tongue, and their noses touched for a lingering moment afterward.

It wasn't until their lips parted that Jake saw Christian's face, and instantly, he recoiled, his mouth opening to scream. But the scream never escaped his lungs, because, just then, he jerked awake in bed, gasping for breath.

The dream was already fading by the time he got to the bathroom and stood before the toilet. He wasn't able to pee right away—he had to work to lose his morning hard-on first. But by the time he flushed, only a hazy memory of the dream remained . . . that final stark image that had awakened him with a jolt.

Christian's face hadn't been human. It had transformed into the face of a white wolf with steel-blue eyes and long, sharp fangs dripping with silvery saliva.

nine

The sun shone brightly on the morning of the third day after the storm, and by the time Jake stepped onto his porch, Christian's Jeep was pulling into the driveway, and Christian was smiling at him through the windshield.

"Breakfast is served," he called out with more gusto than anyone should be able to muster this early in the morning, Jake thought, still rubbing sleep from his eyes. And shortly, they were sitting on Jake's front steps with sausage-and-egg sandwiches on croissant rolls. There were doughnuts and coffee, too. Christian smiled, "Normally, I wouldn't eat this crap twice in a row, but we're gonna burn a lot of calories today, so I guess it's OK. How'd you sleep last night?"

For a crazy half-second, Jake was tempted to tell Christian about the dream in the wheat field, but he just shook his head and said, "Not bad. You?"

"I usually crash like a fuckin' log the second I hit the mattress," Christian said, and took a bite out of his crois-sant. "But last night, it seemed to take forever. Every time I closed my eyes, I kept seeing that crazy chick with the deaf kid and the cat in her car."

The kid wasn't deaf—Jake remembered the girl telling them this, but he didn't bother to correct Christian on the point.

"I don't know when I finally knocked off, but when I woke, I actually thought I dreamed the whole thing." He looked at Jake as he took a sip of coffee. Then, with a raised brow, he asked, "That *did* happen, right? Tell me you saw the same thing. Otherwise, call the men in the white coats to come get me because I'm goin' around the fuckin' bend."

Jake smiled, shaking his head. "You're not going crazy."

Christian laughed. "I mean, what the hell *was* that? Don't get me wrong. She was a pretty hot chick—sort of like Angelina Jolie meets Monica Bellucci, playing some crazy fortune-teller in a wacko David Lynch movie—but what was all that about the kid? I mean, if she was looking for a husband for herself, *I'd* have seriously considered leaving my wife." He chuckled with a wink. "Just kidding, of course. But you know what I mean." He shook his head and took another bite of his sandwich. After washing it down with another swig of coffee, he sighed, "I guess it takes all kinds." Then, he looked to the sky and said, "Looks like we're in for another scorcher. Make sure to hydrate."

They finished breakfast and got straight to work on the back lawns. It took them most of the day just to clear away half of the refuse. They would have kept going into the early evening, except that the dumpster Christian had rented was nearly overflowing.

Christian said, "I should've got the bigger one. I guess I'll have to order another, and have them pick up this one when they drop off the new one."

"I'll get it," Jake said.

Christian shook his head. "Don't worry about it. I've got it covered. You can pick up the tab when we go out for beers after dinner." With a laugh, he added, "Maybe the crazy lady and the mute pretty boy will join us for a round. We'll just have to remember to be on our best behavior. We don't want to piss off the kid's cat and have him turn into a *'toiger'* on us!" He said the last part with a thick accent, and laughed again—a throaty chuckle with a growl, this time. Jake smiled, but his eyes seemed distracted.

They met in Jake's driveway, both showered and dressed, by half past six. Instead of one of his standard camp-collar, short-sleeved linen shirts, Christian was clad in a tight black tank top that showed off his shoulders and arms, and complemented his olive shorts. On his feet, he wore sandals, and around his neck, he wore a bone-colored beaded choker. He smiled at Jake's appraising look and said, "I'm going full Abercrombie tonight. Gotta keep up with Keanu at The Skirt."

"Be careful," said Jake. "I think Keanu likes you."

"That's cool," said Christian. "But if I was gonna swing that way, I wouldn't pick a muscle-buff—it'd be too much like doing it with myself, and even *I'm* not *that* narcissistic!" He chuckled and, with a sly wink and grin, added, "You'd be more my type, anyway." He got in the passenger seat of Jake's BMW. "Come on, fire up this lithium rocket, and let's roll. I'm starving."

ten

Neither of them expected to see anyone from the previous night (save for maybe Keanu, if he happened to be manning the door or waiting tables at The Skirt when they went for drinks after dinner), so they were both a bit surprised when they spotted the kid from The Checkered Skirt on the sidewalk across the street from The Front Grille, Redemption's premiere burger bar. More surprising was that he was alone, and the lady and the cat were nowhere in sight.

Jake supposed he would have just followed Christian inside the restaurant without a second thought, but something happened before they reached The Grille's main entrance. A jet-black Mercedes-AMG GT Roadster with tinted windows pulled up to the curb where the kid stood, and the passenger side window rolled down.

To Jake, it looked like a scene out of a movie—a spooky one, where the innocent ingénue is lured into a car by the unseen killer. The person behind the wheel must have looked friendly because Nacho suddenly smiled. Jake tensed, imagining the door swinging open and the kid getting into the passenger seat, followed by the ear-splitting squeal of tires as the car sped away from the curb with its hostage trapped inside.

But Nacho didn't get in the car (*Not yet anyway*, Jake thought). Instead, he signed something to the driver and pointed in the direction of The Checkered Skirt. Then, the driver must have been talking because Nacho was smiling again and nodding, and he suddenly looked terribly young and innocent.

And vulnerable, Jake thought. Just like the kid who vanishes on the country road at the beginning of countless horror movies, prompting his best friend or sister, or both, to investigate his disappearance and, ultimately, discover him either trapped in a cage in a cobweb-festooned basement of a creepy cult or serial killer . . . or dead in a shallow grave at the climax.

Jake wasn't sure what he was about to do, but two things happened before he could make a move, and they happened almost simultaneously: Nacho stepped toward the car, with that sweet, innocent smile on his face, and a voice called out: "Hey, Nacho—over here!"

Jake was surprised to find that the voice had come from the opposite side of his car, and he was knocked for a loop to see Christian waving the kid over. Nacho's eyes lit up when he saw Christian and Jake, and he quickly signed to the driver, "My friends," and pointed across the street. The driver must have said something like "You sure?" because Nacho nodded and thanked him before heading around the back end of the car and crossing the street at a jog.

He exchanged a greeting with Jake in sign language

and beamed at Christian like a kid encountering a real-life superhero. Jake couldn't fault the boy—Christian did look like a superhero, with his hard body poised and his steely blue eyes gazing after the disappearing taillights of the GT Roadster.

Then, Christian's eyes were on Nacho. "Did you know that guy?"

Nacho shook his head.

"What did he want?"

Nacho shrugged.

"Were you going to get in his car?"

Nacho nodded and signed something before pointing in the direction the car had just gone. Christian didn't need Jake to interpret. The direction was the same as before.

"You were gonna take him to The Checkered Skirt?"

Nacho nodded with an almost heartbreakingly sincere smile. Christian released a sound that fell somewhere between a sigh and a laugh, though he didn't find the situation remotely funny. He shot a look at Jake.

Jake signed, "Where are your friends?"

Nacho furrowed his brow in momentary confusion. Then his smile returned, and he spread his arms to indicate Jake and Christian. The simple gesture, along with the boy's earnest expression, drew unexpected smiles from both of them.

Jake signed, "No. Your *other* friends—from last night—the lady and the cat. Where are they?"

Jake could almost see the bulb lighting above Nacho's head, like in a cartoon. The boy smiled, and his eyes narrowed almost slyly with understanding. Then he made a sweeping upward gesture with both hands and affected a soft exploding sound while waggling his fingers skyward, as if to indicate that his other friends had vanished in a puff of smoke. He looked back at the two men with utmost sincerity.

Jake smiled at this, and Christian almost did, too. But then Christian's face became serious again, and he looked directly into Nacho's eyes. "You can't get into a stranger's car like that. Do you understand me? It's dangerous. You could get hurt."

Nacho gazed at him with a solemn expression. Then he signed something in a rapid series of hand movements that ended with a sweeping gesture toward Christian and Jake. Again, Christian did not require a translation.

"That's different," he said. "You know us from last night." He stopped and thought about it. "OK, we *are* strangers, but we're not *that* kind of stranger." He pointed toward the dark end of the street, where the black GT with the tinted windows had disappeared moments before. "We don't cruise the streets at night looking for kids to get in our car and take us to the local gay bar. Do you understand that?"

Nacho considered thoughtfully for a moment. Then his smile reappeared, and he nodded, making a sign that Christian could not readily decipher.

Christian didn't look to Jake for an interpretation—had he done so, he would have noticed the odd look in Jake's eyes at once, and things might have turned out very differently. Instead, he just smiled, shook his head lightly, and asked, "Are you hungry?" When Nacho nodded in response, Christian tilted his head toward The Grille and said, "Come on."

eleven

They sat in one of the two corner booths at the front of the restaurant with Nacho between them. There was more than enough room for the three of them to spread out on the semicircular padded seat with the extra cushy backing, but Jake noticed how Nacho scooted a little closer to Christian. They ordered burgers, fries, onion rings, and shakes. Christian was going to have the Kobe beef burger with all the trimmings, but when both Jake and Nacho opted for the house veggie burger, he sighed with a grin, "What the hell, let's see if the Impossible is possible."

Nacho had ordered the fries, like Jake, but when the food came, he kept looking at Christian's onion rings, and Christian put the basket between them to share. He made Nacho smile bashfully when he kept stealing a couple of fries from the boy's platter for every ring Nacho took from his basket. Jake smiled, too, and Christian dropped him a wink.

After dinner, Christian and Nacho played two play-er-games in the restaurant's arcade, which was loaded with old-school classics, like Pac-Man, Galaga, Donkey Kong, and Asteroids. They hit them all, but Nacho's favorite by far was Tekken. Nacho worked the controls with speed and dexterity, and won seven out of nine bouts—and he only lost the other two because Christian had shouldered him into laughing and losing his concentration. Jake watched with a smile from the table, thinking how much they seemed like brothers, goofing around and having fun.

When the announcer's voice boomed, "K.O.! MARSHALL LAW WINS!" for the seventh time, Nacho raised his arms in victory with a grin, and Christian gave the boy a double-handed high-five and mussed his hair.

"I give," he said, with a laugh. "You're too good for me. This old man needs a rest." He gave the kid some bills and sent him to get some more tokens.

While Nacho raced to the token dispenser, Christian went back to the table and plopped down across from Jake. "Oh my God, did I ever have that much energy?" He sipped from his shake until the straw rattled at the bottom of the glass and then looked into Jake's eyes. "I don't know what that chick was up to, but that kid isn't nineteen, I can tell you that much. He can't be any older than fifteen. Tops."

Jake had been thinking the same thing since they'd sat down to eat. Outside on the street, he'd guessed the boy could have passed for eighteen—maybe even nineteen, at a quick glance. But here under the warm lights of the restaurant, it was clear that Nacho was a kid.

Jake thought back to the scene outside The Checkered Skirt the night before, trying to remember what the boy had looked like. It had been dark then, too, and Nacho had been partially hidden as he gazed out from the open passenger window of the convertible. The street lamp had seemed muted, leaving half of the boy's face in shadow, like a dramatic shot in an old black-and-white movie. Under such conditions, Jake supposed he could have easily believed the kid was older. But almost *three years* older than he actually was? Jake didn't think so.

Jake looked at Nacho and was about to say something when Christian beat him to the punch. "Well, we can't just leave him here. We'll have to find that crazy Russian chick or whatever she is." He looked at Nacho playing Centipede in the arcade now, and a sadness touched his eyes. "How does somebody do it—dump a kid like that in the street to fend for himself?"

Jake didn't respond. He just watched the boy working the joystick and control buttons with the fevered concentration of a pro gamer. And again, he was struck by how much the kid reminded him of a younger Christian. Not in the face or the body. The young woman who smelled of gypsy water had been correct about that: the kid looked more like a younger version of Jake—lean and angular, with his boyish good looks and tumble of messy, dark hair hanging in his eyes.

But the eyes were different.

The eyes were open and filled with hope and wonder at what the future might hold.

Though the color was close, the boy didn't have Jake's eyes.

He had Christian's eyes.

twelve

They drove by The Skirt to see if the young woman was there, but all they found was the regular crowd, some sitting at the patio tables, others entering and exiting the front doors. Keanu was on duty, but he wasn't covering the entrance—the dance crowd wasn't there in force tonight. Keanu saw them and tipped his head back in greeting. "You guys coming for drinks?"

Christian shook his head and called back, "Maybe later. We're looking for someone—that chick in the blue dress from last night. You remember her?"

Keanu shook his head and smiled with slightly narrowed eyes. "You sure she's a chick?"

Christian laughed. "Positive."

Keanu said, "I'll keep an eye out, let you know if I see her . . . if you stop by for drinks later." He looked at Nacho in the back seat and raised a brow. "Another kid brother?"

Christian looked over his shoulder at Nacho and then back at Keanu with a half-sigh and half-smile. "For tonight, I guess."

Keanu smiled, "Cute kid. Looks just like Lochy."

For a second, Christian was confused. Then he remembered that Keanu didn't know Jake's real name. He looked from Jake to Nacho, who was presently engrossed in a video game on Jake's phone, and nodded. "Yeah, he does."

Keanu winked. "Does he like nachos? If you come back, I'll set you up with a basket on the house. He's too young to go inside, but he can sit with you on the patio."

Christian nodded. "Cool, man. Thanks."

Before Jake pulled away, Keanu asked, "You guys check out The Flamingo yet? Your girl might be there. And your little brother will love it. The fairways will be lit up soon. It's like neon nirvana there."

The woman was nowhere to be found outside The Flamingo, but Nacho's eyes lit up at the sight of all the neon beyond the gates.

Christian turned to Jake with a guilty look and said, "It's like taking a kid to a candy shop and not letting him inside for a taste." Then, with a pouty smile and a sly wink, he added, "Come on, you know you want to." He craned his neck to look at the boy in the back seat. "You wanna go in and play nine holes, Nach, or maybe even the full eighteen?"

The boy nodded enthusiastically, still gazing at the colorful lights.

Christian looked at Jake and affected a whiny childlike croon. "Come on, Dad, *please* . . . "

Jake half-smiled, shaking his head with a sigh. He didn't imagine they would find the woman they were looking for on the neon-lit fairways, chipping long shots across the pond and into the gaping mouth of the big clown head, or putting glow-in-the-dark golf balls up the strobe-lit tunnel of slowly slicing windmills on the eleventh hole. But one look at Nacho's expectant eyes in the rear-view mirror sold him.

In the clubhouse, they selected their clubs and balls. Christian let Nacho pick first. The boy chose a turquoise ball with hazel flecks. Christian took a red ball, and Jake took a purple one. But before they could turn and head for the checkout counter, Nacho waved his hands emphatically while shaking his head. He took both of their balls back and exchanged them for a blue one and a green one with gold and brown flecks. He gave the blue one to Christian, pointing first at the ball and then at Christian's eyes. He handed the green ball to Jake and made the same comparison between his eyes and the ball. Christian nodded with a smooth grin and said, "Color coded. Good idea."

At the counter, Christian waved off Jake's attempt to pay. "Loser pays for ice cream after."

Jake asked, "What if I don't lose?"

Christian shook his head and rolled his eyes with a muted version of his standard high-pitched laugh. "Keep that dream alive, bro."

They played all 18 holes, goofing and laughing a lot on the Front 9. When Jake overshot the 5th hole, and his ball ricocheted off the deck of the Barnacle Barge on the Rapid River and went sailing into the parking lot, Christian and Nacho nearly collapsed with laughter.

Their laughter continued as the three of them searched the parking lot for Jake's ball. When they came up empty-handed, Christian went to the clubhouse, explained what had happened, and got a new ball for Jake. By the time they returned to the course, the laughter had subsided, and by the time they reached the Back 9, both Jake and Christian had settled into "competition mode," shaving extra strokes off their game. Nacho noticed this and followed suit, trying to mimic both of their stances and swings while still keeping up the spirit of the game.

When Jake birdied on the twelfth hole—a particularly difficult one, due to the water hazard that cut a swath straight across the green in front of the hole—Christian nodded appreciatively and said, "Nice wings on that one, bro."

But then, on the same hole, Christian made a double eagle and winked with a sly grin at Jake. Nacho took his time lining up his shot, and it paid off with a hole-in-one. Christian's mouth dropped in shock, and Jake stared in disbelief. The boy had somehow combined both of their techniques to nail the difficult shot.

When Nacho collected his ball and turned to them with a haunting hybrid of Jake's smile and Christian's sly grin on his handsome face, both men cracked up, and Christian hooked an arm around the kid's shoulder, pulling him into a gentle headlock and messing his hair. "Are you hustling us, kid? Is that what this is?" He winked at Jake and said conspiratorially, "I think we might have to make him walk the plank off the Barnacle Barge."

At one of the outside tables, Christian tallied up the scores. Nacho's hole-in-one on the twelfth gave him the win over Christian, who placed second, while Jake came in a not-too-distant third.

Christian grinned at Jake and said, "I'll have the Americone Dream in a sugar cone, please. How 'bout you, Nach?" Nacho nodded, signing that he would have the same. "Double scoops?" Nacho nodded again exuberantly. "That's my boy," Christian said, ruffling Nacho's hair. Then, snapping his fingers at Jake, he said, "Speed it up, loser." Nacho snapped his fingers, too, and made the "L" sign for loser with a playful grin. Jake smiled as he headed for the concession stand.

When he returned to the table, with the two cones for Christian and Nacho and a cup of vanilla ice cream for himself, Nacho was shaking his head stubbornly and signing to Christian, asking for the pencil and the scorecard. Christian gave them to him, and Nacho scratched out his nickname at the top and penciled in the name "Lochy." His print was tight and neat, very like Jake's, except for the first letter, which he wrote in a swirling "L," the same way Christian did with capital letters.

Christian looked down at the card curiously and then up into the boy's earnest eyes. He hadn't used the fake names he'd given Keanu back at The Checkered Skirt. He'd just written his and Jake's real names on the scorecard.

Nacho signed that *he* wanted a real name, too.

When Jake pointed out that he already had a real name—Dzhokhar—Nacho rolled his eyes, making a sour face and shaking his head. He tapped Christian's name on the card and pointed to Christian. Then he tapped Jake's name and pointed to Jake. And finally, with emphasis, he tapped the name he'd penciled on the card above the one he'd scratched out, and, with utmost sincerity, double-thumped his chest.

This sort of reminded Jake of a young gorilla attempting to assert his virility in the presence of dominant simians, and he had to suppress a smile. For a second, he wondered why the boy had chosen the name "Lochy" for his "real name."

The answer came to him suddenly, like a velvet blow, as he recalled the moment with Keanu outside The Checkered Skirt only an hour ago.

Another kid brother?

For tonight, I guess.

Cute kid. Looks just like Lochy.

Before Jake could say anything, Christian nodded thoughtfully and said, "You want to be Lochy now?"

The boy's answer surprised both Christian and Jake. Nacho shook his head and signed, "Not now. Later."

Christian smiled and said, "OK, buddy. You let us know when you want the name change to go into effect."

They ate their ice creams at the table and then took a walk along the lakeside path. Nacho stayed close by, nudging playfully into Christian's shoulder until he spotted the swans on the water ahead and raced to see them up close. Christian smiled at the boy's careful approach toward the water's edge and the gleam in his eyes as he gazed out at the swans. Other kids his age might throw rocks or try to scare the birds off. But Nacho looked upon them with near-reverence, almost as if he'd never seen a swan before.

For a long moment, they both watched from the railing. Then, Jake broke the silence. "What do we do if we can't find her?"

Christian didn't respond. He just kept watching Nacho watching the big birds. They were circling out there on the water under the moonlight. Christian thought he'd read something about swans being diurnal birds, but he couldn't remember. Either way, the two swans that had captured Nacho's attention seemed perfectly content on the dark lake.

"I mean, he's clearly underage," Jake continued. "Might be here on a student visa—most likely an expired one—so, we should probably call someone—"

Jake halted when Christian hit him with an incredulous look and then gave a strange chuckle that ended in a soft half-snort. "What? You want to turn him in? Call ICE?"

Jake looked suddenly cowed. "No. I just—" He sighed. "I mean, he's a kid, and we have a responsibility to make sure he's safe."

"Yeah, and we can do that without calling in the brute squad. Let's not get ahead of ourselves here." He laughed, but not like Jake had said something funny. "There's no reason to call in the cavalry. Like you said, he's just a kid. We can take care of this ourselves."

"Yeah, but if he's not legal—"

"Jesus, listen to yourself!" Christian laughed, but again not like anything was humorous. "Since when do guys like you call kids 'illegal?'" He stopped and lowered his voice. "He's a *person*. People aren't illegal—at least not the last time I checked. And don't even look at me like that. I don't support that sticking-kids-in-cages crap. Those ICE fuckers are the ones who should be locked in cages."

Jake thought about the "Make America Great Again" bumper sticker on Christian's Jeep, and couldn't help feeling the sting of irony. How could anyone put that sticker on his car while being vehemently opposed to one of its core tenets?

But he didn't bring this up to Christian. Instead, he said, "What are we going to do with him if we can't find the girl?"

Christian looked to the dark lake, where streaks of moonlight rippled across its surface as the swans continued their nearly hypnotic circular dance. When he looked back at Nacho, he noticed that the boy was leaning forward with his fingertips stroking the surface of the water in that same circular motion. His nostrils flared slightly as he released a soft breath, and he said, "We'll cross that bridge when we come to it." He paused before adding with no hint of irony, "He never gives us more than we can handle, and we can handle this."

thirteen

Jake drove slowly through the surrounding residential neighborhoods while Nacho sat close to the open window, basking in the warm breeze on his face.

Christian said, "Do any of these houses look familiar to you?"

Nacho shook his head and turned his face back to the window to catch some more breeze time.

Christian gave Jake a look and told him to head for their neighborhood. On Jake's quizzical glance, Christian said, "He's gotta live someplace."

Nacho sat up a little as they pulled into Jake and Christian's neighborhood. When Jake suggested they get out and have a walk around, Nacho's eyes brightened.

They covered the whole block on foot, and when they ended up back at the car, Christian asked, "Did anything look familiar?"

Nacho hesitated and then nodded.

Christian asked, "One of the houses?"

Nacho considered and then nodded again, with a curious smile, this time.

Christian shot a look at Jake and then back at Nacho. "Is this your neighborhood?"

Nacho hesitated again before rapidly signing something that Christian could not decipher. Jake shook his head, indicating that Christian's guess was as good as his.

"I thought you knew sign language, bro."

"I do, but he's using ASL and USL and something else altogether, and I can't—"

Christian cut him off with a sigh and turned back to Nacho, inquiring gently, "Do you know where you live?"

Nacho nodded vigorously and, with a simple yet elegant gesture, indicated the space between Christian and Jake.

Christian sighed with a small smile of exasperation and ruffled the boy's hair. "All right, come on."

They got back in the car and drove to the end of the neighborhood where the lake met the back lawns of the houses on Revenant Road. The moment the houses came into view, Nacho leaned over between the two front seats of Jake's Beemer and pointed through the windshield with a big smile. He signed again, pointing at Jake's house with one hand and Christian's with the other. Then he brought his two forefingers together in a definitive gesture. This time, there was no mistaking his meaning.

Christian nodded and said with a soft laugh, "That's right, buddy. We're home."

fourteen

Both Jake's and Christian's houses were two-storied, but while Jake's had three bedrooms, Christian's only had two—a large master and a sizable yet smaller room, which was to be the nursery. Christian had finished the painting and papering just last month in preparation for the baby's arrival. The only problem was that the storm had blown out the nursery window and destroyed half the room. Christian had sealed the opening where the window had been with a heavy tarpaulin, but the damage was extensive.

Miraculously, the Amish West Estates convertible crib that Marilyn had insisted on buying from DutchCrafters had been spared. The massive oak branch that had skewered the window like a spear hurled by an angry giant had somehow missed the crib altogether. Christian had silently thanked Jesus that the storm had not come *after* the baby was born. He had done this on his knees before the crib with his eyes closed and his head bowed—even though by the time the storm had struck, the point was already moot.

But Christian didn't want to think about that right now. It was still too soon to think about that.

Instead, he concentrated on the situation at hand and said to Jake, "I think it would be best for him to stay at your place for tonight. It's a real mess over at mine. You have a guest room, right?"

Jake nodded.

They were standing on the sidewalk between the two houses, and Nacho was nearby, policing the area around the dumpster where fallen debris still lay. They went to him, and Christian put out a hand to stop the boy from collecting loose scraps and trying to fit them into the over-stuffed bin. "Don't worry about that, buddy. We'll take care of it tomorrow when the new dumpster comes. Let's get you cleaned up and ready for bed. It's been a long day."

Jake took Nacho to the upstairs bathroom and laid a pair of fresh pyjamas on the sink for him. While the boy showered, Jake went down to the kitchen. He found Christian looking out the window at the ruins of the back lawns and the lake beyond, where debris still floated in and bumped against the shoreline like the aftermath of a ship-wreck in some tale he'd read as a boy.

Before Jake could voice his concern, Christian spoke as if reading his mind, "We'll look for her again tomorrow. She can't have gone far. We'll find her . . . "

Jake was silent for a second before asking, "Who do you suppose she is?"

Christian shook his head, still gazing out at the lake.

"I mean, do you think they're related?"

Christian turned to look at him, a mild question mark in his eyes.

"He looks a bit like her," Jake said. "Not like a brother. More like he could be a cousin . . . or a nephew or something."

Christian's eyes narrowed dubiously. "A nephew that she's trying to pimp out to strangers?"

"I don't know," Jake said with a shrug. "Maybe that's not what she was trying to say."

"She was asking you to *marry* him for a green card, dude!"

But Jake wasn't so sure about that anymore. It was possible that they had misheard what the girl had said. It had all come at them so fast, and her accent had been very thick. Maybe they had only *thought* that she was offering the kid up for marriage.

While Christian continued to stare out at the lake like a sentry on vigil, Jake delved deeper into his memory of the night outside The Skirt when the young woman had approached them, and her words came back to him.

She hadn't asked him if he was looking for *a* husband. She had asked if he was looking to *be* a husband.

Are you looking to be husband?

And this question hadn't been directed solely at Jake. Her eyes had shifted from Jake to Christian with anticipation . . . and something else, Jake thought. For just a moment there, as she gazed at him from her place behind the railing on the sidewalk, Jake thought he might have glimpsed a hint of desperation in her eyes. And then, just as quickly, the look was gone, and she'd returned to her matter-of-fact way of speaking, like a door-to-door solicitor delivering a well-practiced sales pitch.

But it was the *other* thing she had said about marriage

that gave Jake pause and made him question her true intention for the boy.

Good match. You marry, keep boy. Two dads. Is all legal now, man to marry man, yes? Be happy. Live long, happy life.

Jake didn't mention any of this to Christian. Instead, they discussed the next day's work. Christian said the replacement window for the nursery would be arriving in the morning and that he and Jake could put it in before finishing the lawn cleanup and getting started on the roof. Jake didn't bother suggesting they hire a professional roofer again—Christian's roof had taken the brunt of the damage from the storm, and it was his decision how he wanted to handle the repairs. He just nodded and said, "Cool. I'm in."

When Nacho came down to the kitchen, showered and dressed in a pair of Jake's pyjamas, he headed straight for the cabinet where Jake kept the glasses. He selected a tall one and poured a glass of water at the sink. Jake was about to tell him how to switch the lever on the faucet for the filtered water, but the boy did it without thinking, as if it were as natural as turning on the tap. Then he went to the cabinet where Jake kept the fig bars and took one out of the sealed container. While he ate his fig bar at the sink, Christian smiled at Jake.

"It's amazing how that skinny body can pack away all that food and still have room for more." He called across the kitchen to Nacho. "Just that one. You don't want to load up before bedtime, buddy."

Nacho nodded and finished his fig bar before downing almost the entire glass of water in a long, continuous swallow that sent his Adam's apple bobbing up and down in a rhythmic dance. Jake reached for the glass, but Nacho turned and placed it inside the dishwasher, effortlessly unlatching the door that had taken Jake forever to figure out how to open after Marc had installed the unit the previous year.

Everything was fine until Christian bid them goodnight and headed for the door. Nacho, who was headed for the stairs, turned back at once and stepped in front of the foyer door. He held out a hand, with his palm flat against Christian's chest, and then began signing and pointing upstairs.

Christian didn't need a translation, but Jake provided it. "He thought you were staying over."

Christian put a hand on the boy's shoulder. "It's OK, buddy. My bed is next door. You're gonna stay here with Jake tonight, and we're all gonna have breakfast together in the morning."

Nacho signed that Christian could stay—or maybe it was *should* stay. The boy signed so rapidly with that confounding combination of ASL and USL—along with all those extra flourishes that didn't come from either—making it almost impossible to keep up with him. As near as Jake could tell, Nacho was saying that they could all stay in the same place, like brothers ... only something must have gotten lost in translation because Jake didn't think that the boy meant to say "brothers"—not precisely anyway.

Christian was still trying to explain the situation, but the boy stood resolutely in front of the door. He pointed at both men and then pressed a palm against his own chest in the same gesture that Jake was pretty sure meant something close to but not quite "brothers." Indeed, the boy's stance was so set and rigid that it reminded Jake of a stubborn dog or cat fixed on something that no one else can see. But Nacho's eyes were fixed on Christian, and after a moment, Christian's blue eyes lost some of their steel, and his mouth curled into a gentle smile.

"All right, all right, I'll stay," he said. "But first, I gotta go home to take a shower." He headed for the door once again, but Nacho took his hand and pulled him up the stairs, nearly tripping over the pant legs of Jake's pyjama bottoms.

When they reached the upstairs hallway, Nacho pointed to the bathroom where he'd recently showered, and Christian laughed. "But my clean clothes are next door—"

Nacho waved like this was no problem at all and made a sweeping gesture at the pyjamas he'd borrowed from Jake, and then pointed at Christian with another sweeping gesture.

Christian laughed again. "I don't think Jake's pyjamas are going to fit me, buddy."

But Nacho was pushing him toward the bathroom and pointing at the shower. When Christian still resisted, Nacho stopped pushing and pinched his nose shut, waving his free hand extra dramatically as if to dispel the odor emanating from Christian. In truth, Christian didn't smell at all, but Nacho's gesture brought a fresh bray of laughter from him, and while he was laughing, it was easy for the boy to shove him into the bathroom and close the door. Christian did not attempt to resist further. He simply called out to Jake, "Do you have a pair of boxers or swimming trunks, bro?"

Jake said he did and that he'd put them on the sink.

Twenty minutes later, Christian came out of the

bathroom, showered and dressed in a pair of Jake's Bermuda shorts (Jake had also left him an oversized T-shirt, but Christian didn't put it on; he always slept shirtless in warm weather).

He padded down the hall to the open master bedroom door. Jake stood at the bedside in his pyjama bottoms and a T-shirt, setting the alarm clock. His hair was still damp from the shower he'd taken in the master bath while Christian was cleaning up in the main bath. Christian was about to ask which room Nacho was in so he could say goodnight when the toilet in the master bath flushed, and then the sink taps were running.

Shortly, Nacho came from the master bath and hopped onto the bed like a kid. He got under the covers in the middle of the king-sized bed and patted the mattress on either side of him with a big smile.

Christian couldn't help laughing and thinking, *How the hell could we have thought he was fifteen? He can't be any older than thirteen, tops.*

Jake shook his head. "I tried to show him the guest room . . . "

Christian looked at Jake and then did something completely unexpected. He dived onto the bed like a kid at a slumber party, and Nacho laughed his soundless laugh, delighted.

"Come on, dude," Christian said, still smiling. "If we're doing a sleepover, we gotta do it right. There's plenty of room for all of us. Hop on in."

Nacho patted the bed again and smiled brightly.

Jake hesitated a moment. Then he set the alarm clock back on the nightstand, turned out the lamp, and climbed into bed. As Jake pulled his end of the covers over himself, Nacho curled up between the two men contentedly and, within a few short minutes, drifted off to sleep.

They lay in the darkness for a time, both of them still and silent on either side of the boy, whose breath now issued in soft waves, like the tide caressing the shore after a storm.

Then, Christian spoke softly. "I'll just stay for a while, bro. Until we're sure he's asleep. Then, I'll head back to my place."

Jake wanted to say something like, "It's cool. You can just stay here." But he didn't. He remained silent in the dark. And sometime later, as he drifted off—not knowing if two hearts were still beating in the bed beside him—the young woman's words came back to him as if in a dream: *You must trust the white wolf—is only one who can protect boy when kotchka is off running.*

fifteen

Sunlight reflected brightly off the lake on the fourth day after the storm. Jake didn't know if Christian had remained throughout the night or gone back to his own house sometime before dawn. But Nacho was the only one in bed with him when he woke. The boy was fast asleep, curled up close to the pillow Christian had used the night before.

Jake rolled over and looked at the alarm clock, surprised to find that it was half past nine. He'd set it for six-thirty; he was sure of that (Christian was an early riser, and Jake had gotten used to his schedule over the past few days). Still, he felt sleepy and closed his eyes, curling into his pillow. He'd had the strangest dreams last night; the remnants of the final one came back to him now.

In the dream, he had been walking through the Iowa wheat field again . . . only this time, the wheat had been neatly mown or scythed or whatever farmers do to it, creating paths between its tall, waving tillers, like a maze. In the distance ahead, a boy of no more than eleven was racing through the wheat maze, barefoot and clad only in a pair of baggy khaki shorts with big cargo pockets, his tanned skin glowing in the radiant sun.

The boy was followed by a cat with patchy markings and a large white dog with steely blue eyes. At first, Jake had thought the boy was racing from these animals, who broke off in separate directions to head him off and catch him before he could escape the wheat maze.

Jake started after them, but soon realized it was just a game of hide-and-seek the three were playing. The cat and dog first cornered the boy and then leapt at him, the cat nudging his head under the boy's chin, the dog pelting the boy's face with kisses while the boy laughed soundlessly.

Jake stopped and watched, his heart still hammering from the run, when a familiar voice whispered in his ear: *They will protect him with their lives . . . but need you . . . make good marriage . . . two dads . . . long, happy life . . . trust the white wolf . . . kotchka will follow . . .*

And the voice whispered one more thing: *Wake now . . . boy hungry . . . feed him.*

Jake opened his eyes to an aroma he hadn't smelled in this house since Marc had been here. Jake had never been a good cook. To him, breakfast was cereal, toast, and coffee. Marc had been the master of the hot morning meals, and he had prepared them regularly enough for Jake to feel a strong surge of nostalgia at the aroma presently wafting up the stairwell from the kitchen.

Jake pulled on a T-shirt as he came downstairs, barefoot and clad in jeans. Christian smiled at him from the stove where he was making biscuits and gravy and scrambled eggs. Nacho was already at the table with a tall glass of orange juice and a bright smile. Jake took the seat across from him.

"Just on time," Christian said, setting two steaming plates on the table before Nacho and Jake. As Jake breathed in the delicious aroma, Christian added with a wink, "Best alarm clock in the land. Guaranteed to wake you up on time, and with a smile, every morning."

Jake thought of asking Christian if he had turned off the alarm clock before leaving last night or early this morning, so he would have enough time to go shopping and prepare this meal. But he stayed quiet. He'd needed the extra sleep and so had Nacho.

Christian asked, "Coffee, juice, or both?"

"Coffee," Jake said. Christian poured two cups and brought them to the table before getting his own plate from the stove and taking the seat between Jake and Nacho. Jake was a bit surprised when both Christian and Nacho dug right in. With the formal breakfast spread and a guest, he'd half-expected Christian to say grace, or at least bow his head for a brief moment of silence. Of course, Christian had never said grace before any of their other meals—but those had been out on the driveway with egg croissants and doughnuts from Dunkin' or at restaurants, like The Front Grille, where even the most religious of people didn't offer prayers before eating.

The dryer in the mud room off the kitchen chimed just as they were finishing up breakfast. "I washed his clothes before I went to the market and put them in the dryer when I got back. Hope you don't mind. I still don't have power at my place because I'm one of those stubborn Repubes who failed to get on board with the solar panels. Though how your little green roof-warts survived that storm is beyond me."

Jake smiled at the quip—he knew Christian was just ribbing him—and collected the plates and glasses for the dishwasher while Christian retrieved Nacho's clothes from the dryer.

The table was cleared and the dishwasher was halfway through its first cycle when Nacho came down from the bathroom with his teeth brushed (Christian had picked up a toothbrush for him when he'd gone to get the things for breakfast) and his clean clothes on. He left his flannel and hoodie on Jake's bed and just wore his jeans and his T-shirt with the Green Day logo. He sat on the bottom riser of the stairs to lace up his Chuck Taylor Converse sneakers, which Christian had also washed and set to dry on the patio out back of Jake's house.

When the boy stood, ready and eager to take on the day's clean-up duties with the guys, Jake noticed how his jeans sagged on his hips. He'd thought they would be tighter after their recent run through the washer and dryer. But they seemed even looser than they had the night before. Nacho kept hiking them up and smiling apologetically.

Jake got a braided belt from his closet, weaved it through the loops of Nacho's jeans, and cinched it with a nod of approval. Nacho pinched at the shoulders of his T-shirt, tugged outward twice, and smiled smartly with sly eyes, like a boy going off to his first formal rather than a kid off to clear away the debris from a recent storm.

Jake smiled, too. But his eyes looked curious because Nacho's T-shirt also appeared to hang a bit looser on him than it had the night before.

sixteen

The window for the nursery arrived shortly after nine, and with Nacho's help, they had it installed within a half hour. Nacho was particularly proud of this achievement and marveled at the casement's sleek design and smooth action as he opened and closed it several times. He signed to Christian and made a sweeping gesture to indicate the rest of the house.

"Yeah, you're right," Christian said with a laugh. "We should probably swap out the rest of the windows and start off fresh. But first, we've got to clean up that mess outside and take care of the roof before it starts leaking." He ruffled the boy's hair. "Otherwise, we'll *all* have to live at Jake's house."

Nacho nodded with a serious expression, and his hands were moving again. It took only a moment for Christian to glean the meaning. The boy indicated two houses coming together as one, and in this single house, there was a big bed with three people sleeping in it.

"Yeah, but that was a special occasion, buddy. If we did a sleepover every night in Jake's California king, it wouldn't be special, you know?"

Nacho signed again, making the image of *two* beds this time, one large and the other small. Then, as if to clarify his meaning, he pointed at the Amish convertible crib.

Christian laughed. "I think I might be too big for that bed, buddy."

Nacho rolled his eyes with a crooked smile and shook his head as if Christian was being silly. He waved a hand and mimicked scratching out the notion of Christian sleeping in the crib. Then, he pressed his hand to his own chest and nodded at the crib.

Christian gave him a narrow-eyed look, with a thin but good-humored smile, and said, "I think you might be a little too big for it, too."

Christian and Jake collected the scraps from the window job and pitched them out the open window into the dumpster in the driveway below, and Nacho joined them . . . but his eyes kept returning to the crib with a speculative gleam.

After the nursery was squared away, Christian suggested that Jake and Nacho start on the backyard cleanup while he tackled the roof. The plan was settled until Christian hauled out the ladder from his garage, and Nacho realized that "tackling the roof" meant going up the ladder and actually being *on* the roof. He rapidly signed his interest, pointing up at the roof and then at himself and Christian. Jake was dubious and started to say something, but Christian smiled with a glance up the ladder.

"You think you're up to being my apprentice?"

Nacho nodded eagerly.

"OK, but you have to listen carefully and obey all my instructions. No clowning around or horseplay. This is serious stuff. It's high up there, and you could get hurt. You understand?"

Nacho nodded solemnly.

Jake opened his mouth to protest. "Maybe he should just stay down here with me—"

Christian said, "It's all good. It's not very steep up there. He'll be all right." And to Nacho, he said, "Let's get you padded up. Safety first."

Nacho nodded solemnly again, but couldn't suppress the smile curling at one corner of his mouth. He wanted to be up where the sun was bright and the branches of the tall oak overhung the roof like the fingers of giants. Christian fitted him with knee and elbow pads while Jake watched, again struck by how the two seemed like brothers.

The boy went for the ladder as soon as the pads were secured, but Christian called for him to come back immediately.

Jake breathed a sigh of relief, thinking Christian had changed his mind about taking the kid up on the roof with him. But Christian hadn't changed his mind. He bent to one knee and told Nacho to hold still. Nacho complied while Christian cuffed his jeans.

"Can't have you tripping over these. Jake'll have my hide if you take a tumble off that roof." He winked at Jake, and Jake managed a small smile. Christian caught the apprehension in his eyes and said, "Don't worry. He'll be fine. Damage probably isn't that bad up there. We'll be up and down in a jiff. I'll keep an eye on him. I promise."

Christian turned out to be right about the damage. It was minimal—the worst part was the flashing by the chimney, and even that was a breeze to repair. But he was wrong about the other thing. Nacho wasn't the one who needed a guardian eye on him up on the roof.

They had been at it for a couple of hours, and most of the damage was repaired. Christian had shown Nacho how to properly remove damaged tiles and clean the area beneath them before laying down a fresh sheet of rubberized asphalt and placing new tiles. Nacho listened attentively and executed every step with diligence and precision.

When the sun came over the house at noon, Christian stripped off his T-shirt and made it into a head wrap, covering his hair. He smiled when Nacho did the same and helped the boy secure it properly. Nacho smiled back and hoisted his "guns," flexing both. Christian laughed and flexed his infinitely more stacked set of "armament." Nacho's eyes instantly widened, and he pointed at the birthmark on the inside of Christian's left upper arm. Though not very large and relatively unremarkable, the birthmark had grabbed the boy's attention, and suddenly, he was signing rapidly and excitedly.

Christian didn't have a clue what the boy was trying to tell him until Nacho lifted his own arm and pointed at the birthmark on the inside curve of his bicep. It was located in the same spot as Christian's.

Christian examined Nacho's birthmark and then lifted his own arm for comparison. Nacho looked with him and finger-spelled the word, "SAME."

Christian studied the two birthmarks at length. Then, a slow, smooth grin spread across his face, and he nodded. Save for their size, the two birthmarks were otherwise nearly identical: a dot above a squiggle, giving the mark the appearance of an inverted semicolon. Christian ruffled the boy's hair and said, "It's our superhero symbol. We're The Defenders." Then he put a finger to his lips and said, "We have to keep it a secret and only tell people that we really trust."

Nacho pointed at Jake, who was clearing away scraps down on the lawn, and with a sincere look in his eyes, signed a question mark.

Christian said, "Of course! Jake's our boy." He looked over the roof's edge and then back at Nacho with a confidential wink. "We'll just have to break it to him gently. He doesn't have the mark, and he might be a bit jealous at first."

Nacho broke into a grin. He knew that Christian was only joking about the mark being a superhero symbol. But this didn't stop him from periodically looking at his and Christian's birthmarks with a sense of pride.

They worked side by side until Jake called up from the foot of the ladder that it was time to break for lunch.

Christian called back with a laugh, "As long as *you're* not cooking!"

And that's when it happened.

Christian turned his head to give Nacho a playful wink, but at the same time, he did something stupid—something he'd learned *never* to do back in the days he'd worked summers on a construction crew to earn money for college.

He took a step on a slope without first looking, and his right foot caught a loose tile. At first, he thought he could regain his balance and course-correct, but then the tile slipped from under him, and he was falling backward.

Jake gaped from the lawn below, and in a lucid flash, he could see Christian plummeting backward, arms pinwheeling almost comically (though there was nothing remotely funny about it), and crashing to the ground. Instinctively, Jake raised his arms as if the gesture could somehow stop Christian's backward tumble while his mind raced frantically with one thought: *If you're real, save him—he believes in you, save him . . .*

At the roof's edge, Christian suddenly stopped, his back arched, his arms reaching for purchase in thin air. And then, miraculously, he fell the other way—*toward* the roof instead of off it, as if he were attached to invisible bungee cords which had reached their limit and suddenly recoiled . . . or a heavenly hand had taken hold and pulled him back from the brink.

It turned out to be nothing quite as dramatic or fantastical.

Up on the roof, Nacho had seen what was happening and reacted with the lightning-fast reflexes of an agile teenager. He grabbed Christian's leather utility belt and fell back on his butt, yanking with all his might. Christian fell forward and would have crushed the skinny boy but for his own reflexes. He ended up with his hands planted on the roof to either side of the boy's head. And with closed eyes, he touched his forehead to Nacho's and breathed a sigh of relief.

When they sat up, Christian placed a hand on the back of the boy's neck, gently squeezing, and said softly, "You saved me, buddy, you saved me."

Nacho leaned into Christian's touch and tapped his broad chest twice. Then, he made a fist with his right hand, and with the index and middle fingers of his left hand spread into a V, he moved them forward against the back of his fist. He finished by tapping his own chest and extending his pinky and thumb into a Y, which he moved in a side-to-side motion.

Christian didn't need a translation.

Nacho's meaning was clear: *You saved me, too.*

seventeen

With the three of them working together, the lawn cleanup moved swiftly and efficiently, save for a brief wrestling match between Christian and Nacho after Nacho almost nudged Christian into the lake just so he could "save" him from falling in by grabbing his belt and pulling him back at the last second. Christian chased the boy down, tackling and tickling him for his cheek, and Nacho laughed delightedly. Jake suspected the boy had been "riding the brakes" as he'd run away to ensure that he would be caught and tackled by his pursuer. And when Christian came back with Nacho slung over one shoulder, both of them smiling and out of breath, Jake was sure of it.

They wrapped for the day at five and headed inside to clean up (this time, Nacho didn't dispute Christian showering at his own place). Jake had just come out of the master bath and was toweling off when he heard Christian's Jeep pulling out of the driveway next door.

This didn't surprise Jake. They had let Nacho decide what he wanted for dinner, and he had chosen pizza.

Since Nacho only had one set of clothes that would take at least an hour to launder, Jake assumed that Christian had ordered the pizza and gone to pick it up. While waiting for Christian to return with dinner, Jake rummaged through his dresser for something that might fit the boy. Nacho, fresh from his own shower, sat on the couch in Jake's bathrobe watching cartoons.

Jake raised a curious brow when Christian came through the front door at six with a couple of shopping bags from Abercrombie & Fitch instead of a pizza from Mariano's. Christian set one of the bags on the coffee table in front of Nacho, and as he headed for the kitchen, he called over his shoulder, "Now, don't say I never gave you anything."

Jake was in the kitchen doorway, still looking bemused as Nacho leaned forward with anticipation and peered into the bag. A delighted smile bloomed as he reached inside and retrieved its contents one by one. There were three T-shirts, two short-sleeved linen button-ups (one navy, the other oyster white), a long-sleeved pinstriped A&F Go-To, two pairs of shorts with cargo pockets (one khaki, the other olive, just like the pair Christian had been wearing the night they'd found Nacho wandering the street outside The Front Grille), two pairs of jeans, a bundle of boxers, and a bundle of socks.

Jake watched as Nacho went through the bag like a kid on Christmas morning. "That was some spree," he said.

Christian smiled and shrugged. "You're only young once. Besides, we can't have him running around in clothes that don't even fit." Then he called over his shoulder, "Come on, buddy, time for pizza. Pick something out and get dressed."

While Nacho got dressed upstairs, Jake asked, "What about shoes?"

Christian held up the other bag. "No sweat. Boy Scout's got it covered, Dad."

Nacho came down dressed in the olive cargo shorts, the black T-shirt, and the navy linen short-sleeved button-up with the front open. While Christian laced up the deck shoes and put them on Nacho like a clerk at a shoe store, pressing his thumb against the toe to make sure they fit properly, Jake marveled at Christian's eye—all of the clothing Christian had bought in his quickie shopping spree fit the boy perfectly.

As if reading Jake's thoughts, Christian said, "He's built like you. Classic model frame. Clothes just hang perfectly on him."

Before they headed out, Christian looked Nacho over with a speculative eye and shook his head. "Nah, something's missing."

The boy looked momentarily confused. Then, with a smile, Christian pulled one last item out of the smaller bag, and Nacho's eyes lit up again. The item was a beaded choker, just like Christian's. He placed it around Nacho's neck and fastened the clasp. The boy touched the choker with near-reverence.

Christian smiled at Jake's eye roll. "Come on, bro. You can't deny him a little bling."

They took Christian's Jeep to Mariano's and let Nacho order. When he requested the spinach thin crust, Jake suggested they get two medium pies—one with spinach for Nacho and one with pepperoni for Christian, and he could share with them both. Christian made a face and shook his head.

"You hate meat on your pizza, dude." With a smile, he told the server they'd have a large thin spinach. When Nacho ordered an Orange Crush, Christian and Jake skipped their usual beers and had the same.

After dinner, Christian said that it was "hero's choice" tonight and let Nacho pick the evening's activities. "So what's it gonna be, little hero? More mini golf? Go-carts? Batting cages? The coasters? You name it."

Nacho made an encompassing gesture with a smile, and Jake looked dubious. But Christian nodded with a grin.

"All of the above, eh? Good choice."

They didn't do everything, of course—there wasn't enough time. But they did get a lot in, starting with the batting cages, where they discovered that Nacho was a natural with "a sweet stance, a sharp eye, and a powerful cut," as Christian put it. From there, they hit most of the carny rides on the Boardwalk, including the massive Ferris wheel, which Nacho absolutely adored because it felt like flying.

After the carny rides, they hit two of the biggies—the Iron Dragon, a steel coaster with a couple of tight corkscrews and a generous loop, and the Raptor, a massive out-and-back wooden coaster that coiled into itself multiple times before careening into a generous curve at the north end of the Boardwalk and bulleting back to the south end where it had started.

They closed out the evening with the gaming booths on Gallery Row. Christian impressed both Jake and Nacho with his skill at the shooting gallery, bagging seventeen of the twenty tin targets in a row (and he only missed the first three because he used them to gauge the rifle's sight).

The old-timer behind the booth whistled low and said,

"The last time I saw somebody shoot like that was in the movies! Pick your prize. Anything on the top shelf."

Christian turned to Nacho, raising a brow. "You heard the man."

But Nacho didn't want any of the top-shelf prizes, which were stuffed animals almost as big as he. Instead, he pointed at one of the lower shelves with a tentative yet hopeful look in his eyes.

"You sure?" Christian asked.

Nacho nodded and pointed at a stuffed elephant three tiers down from the top row. It was about the size of a football and had soft grey fur with small black eyes. Nacho signed, "For the baby."

It was a simple statement that anyone could get, and the old-timer hooked down the prize and handed it to Nacho. With a smile and wink at Christian and Jake, he said, "He's a good big brother, thinking of the little one at home."

Jake looked nonplussed at first, and then the image of the crib in the nursery at Christian's place surfaced, and he returned the old-timer's smile. Christian smiled, too, but not his full smile. For a moment, he looked about a thousand miles away. But then, Nacho was tugging him toward another gaming booth—a bottle-toss game, where to win, you had to knock down six stacked bottles with a baseball.

"This one?" Christian asked. "You sure?"

Nacho nodded and tapped the counter for Christian to lay down the money. Christian took a five-dollar bill off his roll and placed it in front of the barker manning the booth, a kid of sixteen or seventeen in the purple Pier Playland employee T-shirt. The kid had a tight build and would have been good-looking, Christian supposed, if not for the explosion of acne on his forehead and chin, and one whopper of a blackhead on the left side of his nose.

But that's not what bothered Christian about him. It was the sneaky set of his eyes and the subtle grin he sported as he set three balls on the board for Nacho. To Christian, he looked like an elf—and not an elf of the *Lord of the Rings* variety. He looked more like the kind of elf that hides under a bridge waiting for a kid like Nacho to happen along.

There's a fee for crossing this bridge, kid, those slightly strabismal eyes of his seemed to say.

But Nacho didn't notice any of this. He was focused on the three sets of stacked bottles as he picked up the first baseball and pondered its weight. Then, like a pitcher on the mound, he executed a perfect windup and threw a clean fastball straight and sure. It knocked over every bottle in the first pyramid.

Christian beamed with pride.

The teen behind the counter smiled his elvish smile as the strange cast in his right eye caught the overhead light and appeared to glint with a hint of disdain. "Two more like that, and the top tier is yours, kid."

But to Christian's ear, it sounded more like: *There's a fee for crossing this bridge, kid.*

Nacho took the second ball, squared off, wound up, and pitched, same as before—a fastball, straight through the strike zone. The shot took down all the bottles, save for one. It rocked on its base, but remained standing precariously balanced on the edge of the pedestal.

Jake looked impressed, but Christian was looking at the ghost of a grin playing at one corner of Pizza Puss's zit-flecked mouth. He was about to say something—just what, he didn't know—when the last bottle, still dubiously perched, fell off the edge of the pedestal and clunked to the ground with a hollow thud.

This time, the gleam of disdain in Pizza Puss's strabismal eyes was plain to see. But he smiled as he announced, "One more, and you got it, kid."

Right down here under my bridge.

Nacho took the last ball and wound up for the pitch. Jake tensed. But before the ball was released, Christian thought calmly and clearly, *No breaking ball, buddy. Changeup pitch. Nine miles slower than your best. Nice and easy, straight through the strike zone.*

The pitch looked like it was going to be another 4-seam fastball with a break, but the velocity was nine miles slower than Nacho's fastest . . . and it swept straight through the strike zone, knocking over all six bottles.

Jake smiled. Christian hooked an arm around Nacho's shoulder and pulled him into a one-armed embrace, kissing him on the top of his head and saying, "That's my boy!"

Pizza Puss released a soundless sigh, shaking his head with a grin that may or may not have been grudging—it was hard to tell with that strange cast in his right eye—and said, "Good job. Top tier, kid. Any one you want."

Again, Nacho didn't go for one of the prizes at the top. Instead, he pointed to the third tier from the bottom, where the woven embroidery floss friendship bracelets hung, held up two fingers, and made a question mark. Pizza Puss didn't have any trouble understanding. He just shook his head, with a genuine smile this time, and chuckled, "Why not? Why the heck not? Any color preference, kid?"

Nacho pointed, and Pizza Puss hooked two bracelets for him—one green-and-yellow, the other blue-and-red.

Nacho gave the green-and-yellow one to Christian and

the blue-and-red one to Jake. Christian said with a kind laugh, "I think you got your colors mixed up, buddy."

Nacho shook his head and signed something that didn't make sense. On the quizzical glances of Jake and Christian, Nacho pointed to the bracelet he'd given to Christian and indicated Jake's left wrist. He did the same with the bracelet he'd given to Jake, indicating Christian's right wrist. Christian nodded with a smile and put the green-and-yellow bracelet around Jake's wrist, tying it off with a fixed knot. At Nacho's insistence, Jake did the same, securing the blue-and-red bracelet around Christian's wrist.

Then, Christian winked and said, "I guess it's official. We're married."

eighteen

They took one last spin on the Ferris wheel before heading to Christian's Jeep. It was quarter to midnight, and the evening had pretty much drained them all. But it was a good tired feeling after a long day of work and play. The ride home was quiet. Christian put on some mellow tunes, and by the time they pulled into Jake's driveway, Nacho was fast asleep in the back seat.

Christian killed the engine, and before Jake could say anything, he was out of the car and opening the back door. He unbuckled the seatbelt, took the boy into his arms, and effortlessly carried him into Jake's house. Nacho stirred but didn't wake when Christian put him on the bed in Jake's guest room and removed his shoes and socks, along with the cargo shorts and the linen shirt. Then, he tucked the boy under the blankets in his T-shirt and boxers. There was no nightlight in the room, so Christian left the door open a crack, with the hallway dimmer set on low.

Down in the kitchen, Jake didn't mention anything

about them not looking for the young woman tonight, but Christian spoke as if he had. "We'll look for her tomorrow. The kid needed a break today." He paused, looking out the window at the darkened lake, and said softly, "What does it matter if we don't find her anyway? It's pretty obvious that she dumped him." He halted for a second, but still didn't look at Jake. "I mean, what're we gonna do—hand him back over to her so she can try to sell him to somebody else?"

Jake's lips parted. He was about to say that the woman hadn't asked for money, but thought better of it. The look in Christian's eyes told him that now wasn't the time to reason with him.

Christian released a breath through his nose and spoke softly again, "He can stay with us for now. There's no rush. He likes it here. He's happy. Let's just leave it at that for now, OK?"

Jake was about to respond, but abruptly stopped when Christian's eyes shifted from the window and lit upon him. Under the dim light over the kitchen sink, Christian looked a lot like Marc. Jake had never really thought of this before, but it was true. Christian had the same build, the same flawless skin, the same mischievous yet earnest smile as Marc. But it wasn't these similarities between Christian and Jake's ex that caused his heart to flutter and his breath to catch when Christian looked at him, because, in truth, Marc had never caused Jake's heart to flutter or his breath to catch with a simple unexpected glance like that.

Of course, Jake had been *attracted* to Marc—they wouldn't have lasted as long as they had if there hadn't been chemistry between them. And sex with Marc had been good—really good. But something had been missing—some crucial element that makes a relationship not only click but last.

Looking at Christian in the dimly lit kitchen now, Jake felt a crazy impulse to take him by the hand and lead him upstairs to his bedroom.

Marc would have smiled at the notion of Jake taking charge like that. He might have even laughed. In intimate relations, Marc had always been the aggressor. He liked having sex a lot, and it wasn't uncommon for him to do it anywhere in the house when the urge struck. He had once wrapped his arms around Jake from behind in the laundry room, pressing the stiff rod in his pants against Jake's backside and whispering, "I want you now." When Jake tried to move things to the bedroom upstairs, Marc kept unbuttoning his shirt from behind while groaning, "It's too far away. I need it right here, right now."

And so, Jake had stopped folding towels, and they did it right there in the laundry room, with Marc leading every step of the way, and Jake willingly giving in to his every whim. And when it was done, Jake was satisfied—Marc was a very attentive lover and often seemed more concerned with Jake's orgasm than his own. But as satisfying as sex was with Marc, it often felt incomplete. It was almost as if only one of them was involved in the lovemaking while the other was merely a passenger.

This had gone on until the night Jake had stepped out of his comfort zone and asked Marc to do something different. They had just come home from Marc's birthday dinner, and Marc had been ready for sex—he'd been saving it, actually, not approaching Jake for an entire week beforehand, and he was brimming to burst. But before they went inside,

Jake turned off the car in the garage and asked Marc to do something for him.

Marc grinned slyly and said, "But it's *my* birthday."

Jake allowed that it was indeed Marc's birthday and told him precisely what he wanted to give him as a gift.

Marc's sly grin became a curious one. "I'm listening. Proceed, counselor." Marc was a paralegal studying for the bar exam and often used this phrase when he sensed a serious discussion coming on.

Jake told him what he wanted, and after a long moment of silent contemplation, Marc agreed. It wasn't that Jake wanted Marc to cede complete control; he'd just wanted to take the reins at the onset and see if they could meet somewhere in the middle.

It had started off all right, with Marc allowing Jake to lead and even be the more dominant player, and Jake had enjoyed handling Marc's body in ways that Marc normally handled his. He liked it when Marc flexed his muscles while feigning attempts to "break free" and "regain control." Each of these times, Jake would push him back onto the pillow and probe his hard body further. But as things got more intense, Marc's attempts to break free no longer seemed feigned. And his hands no longer seemed satisfied with just reciprocal petting and stroking. He wanted to be on top and back in charge.

The night had ended well, with both Jake and Marc reaching gratifying climaxes. But later, as they lay in the darkness, Marc sensed something was off and spoke softly from his side of the bed.

"If you wanted to be in control, you should have tied me up. I'd be cool with that. I did it a couple of times before

I met you—it can be pretty intense, especially when you come." He paused and sighed through his nose, and his tone shifted. "But you can't expect a guy like me to be submissive without anything to hold him back. It's not in my nature. I'm an alpha. You know that. You've known it since we first met. I can't just lay there and be your bitch. You want that, go to the head shop, get some leather, and do it right. I don't mind doing it with someone I trust. We can do it whenever you want."

Marc's tone had slipped into petulance, and Jake's response came in kind. "I'm not interested in raping you."

"Who said anything about rape?" Marc snapped suddenly. "It's fantasy superhero bondage—and you're obviously into superheroes, otherwise, you wouldn't be here with me." He took a beat, and Jake thought maybe he was going to let it drop. But that wasn't Marc's style; once he was locked and loaded, he almost always emptied the clip. "You wanna worship me, fine. Worship me. But don't expect me to just lay there while you play out your little superhero wet dream. Man up, and do it properly."

They stayed together for two and a half months after that, and the sex continued to be good, but Jake never asked to take the lead again, and one night at dinner, Jake said, "I think we should take a break."

He'd half-expected Marc to put up resistance, maybe even try to coax him up to the bedroom for a reminder of what he'd be giving up. But Marc just nodded, thoughtfully, and three days later, he was packed and gone.

Jake still remembered their goodbye in the foyer. He remembered the sound of a lawnmower in the background of that warm spring day, the smile on Marc's face when he glanced across the hedges at a shirtless Christian Worthing mowing his lawn next door. "Maybe you should give Captain America a shot. He's more wholesome than I am. He's not gonna be your bitch, but he won't put up much resistance when you want to get on top and take charge, either. He's probably a real power-bottom. Perfect for you. Capitulation with strength. Just your speed."

Jake rolled his eyes with a smile. "I don't think that would sit too well with his wife."

Marc laughed with a wink. "I don't think a lot is gonna sit too well with his wife when all the dirty laundry comes out in the wash."

Jake snorted a timid laugh. "He's straight."

And now it was Marc's turn to roll his eyes. "Yep. So was I—all the way through high school and halfway through college. And then I met you." On Jake's curious expression, he laughed. "You think I audited that art class just for Litchfield's golden oratory? The second I saw you on the quad, my pink wings sprouted and spread out wide. I raced back to my dorm and rubbed one out to that photo of you in the registry—the one where you look like a complete yummy dork because somebody convinced you that you had to dress formal for your school ID."

Jake had blushed, but his eyes were still on Christian mowing his lawn, oblivious to the fact that he was being watched by the two gay guys next door.

Or maybe not.

I may not be into guys, but it's still a boost to my ego when I catch one of them checking me out, you know?

Even now, Jake couldn't be sure of it, but it seemed as if Marc had timed his goodbye kiss on the porch—a sweet and lingering one on the lips—to coincide with Christian's long pass by the white picket fence that separated the two lawns. And before he'd headed for his car, Marc had said with a sly but good-natured smile, "Let me know how it turns out with the Cap'n and his Vibranium shield."

In the kitchen, Christian snapped his fingers in front of Jake's eyes and said, "Ground Control to Major Tom."

Jake looked startled and then smiled sheepishly. "Sorry . . . "

"Jesus, bro," Christian laughed, "where did you *go* there? I thought we lost you to deep space!"

Jake shook his head. "Sorry, I . . . "

Christian laughed again, a subdued version of his patented high-pitch laugh, and clapped Jake on the shoulder. "Time for you to hit the sack, buddy. You're zonked. You want me to come up and tuck you in, too?" Another soft, high-pitched laugh. At the door, he said, "Good time. Glad we did it. Now get to bed. We have a full day tomorrow."

Up in his room, Jake stripped to his boxers and climbed into bed. But he didn't go straight to sleep. He was still thinking about Marc and what had led to their split. And then he was thinking about Christian, and what Marc had said about Christian. Marc had never been one of those guys who believe that every hot guy they encounter is a closeted fag waiting for the right fag to come along and coax him out. When Marc had finally worked up the nerve to approach Jake, he knew what he wanted, and he knew that Jake wanted the same thing.

Maybe you should give Captain America a shot. He's more wholesome than I am.

Jake thought about that day Christian was out mowing

his lawn. He thought about *all* the days Christian was mowing his lawn—always shirtless, always with a casual glance up from the mower . . . right at the moment Jake happened to be looking over the fence.

He thought if Christian were gay, things would be different with him than they had been with Marc. He thought Christian would have no problem letting him take charge and explore his body, and after Jake had discovered all the places that stimulated and excited Christian, they would meet in that middle ground he and Marc had failed to find, and something special would happen.

Jake swallowed dryly. He wanted to reach into his boxers and relieve himself while thinking about his next-door neighbor. He suddenly wanted this very badly.

Instead, he lay on his back, and, staring into the darkness above, thought of Marc, whom he had shared this bed with for three years. He didn't imagine himself making love to Marc, because he didn't feel that way toward Marc anymore—in truth, he wasn't sure he had ever felt that way toward Marc. He had enjoyed spending time with him and genuinely cared about him—he even missed him a little. But he wasn't sure that those things amounted to love . . . at least not the sort of love that makes you eager to wake up in the morning and spend another day with him, even if it's just a day of clearing away the debris from a recent storm and then heading out for beers at the local pub afterward.

Jake had one last thought of relieving the itch that had come upon him so suddenly, and he imagined himself with Fantasy Superhero Marc as a one-night pickup—something he had never done before. He imagined himself as Angry Jake, taking complete charge of Superhero Marc for the first time and holding onto the reins for the duration. He was still aroused, but he couldn't make it happen, not even as a quickie fantasy—or what Marc would have called with grinning aplomb, "a revenge fuck"—because he didn't want a fantasy, and he didn't want revenge.

He wanted something more.

He lay there for a long time before turning onto his side and curling into his pillow. And when sleep finally came to claim him, he was no longer thinking of Marc, because that was in the past. He didn't know precisely what the future might hold, but he was content to be here in the present with the hope for something more.

His last thought before drifting off was pure and simple: he was glad that he hadn't given in to the urge to gratify himself while thinking of either Christian or Marc because it would have felt like a betrayal of the friendship and trust that he and Christian had built over the past four days.

nineteen

The sun rose late on the morning of the fifth day after the storm. Jake didn't find this unusual—it was, after all, the twenty-third of September, and despite the continued heatwave, autumn had officially begun the day before.

What he did find unusual was that he'd just now noticed this. It was as if the baton had been handed off overnight instead of the gradual change from summer to fall that typically transpired over the course of weeks.

Jake got out of bed with the rising sun and went to the bathroom before stepping into his jeans and pulling a T-shirt over his head. Usually, he was in no rush to get down to the kitchen, but this morning he moved with a purpose; the aroma of pancakes wafting up the stairwell made his stomach growl with exigency.

Christian was at the stove, pulling the first batch of pancakes from the griddle, and he greeted Jake with his big morning smile. "It'll just be a second. I don't make them like they do in the movies, with a huge stack getting cold on a platter. I do them fresh from the griddle to the plate, piping hot . . . just like my ma and pa used to do back on the farm after they found me in that cornfield as a baby."

He winked at Jake, who instantly blushed, recalling the time Marc had made a joke about Christian being found in an Iowa cornfield in his spacecraft to spread "truthiness, fascism, and the 'Murican way."

Marc had said this while he and Jake were having a beer on the porch one evening. Christian had just gotten out of his Jeep with the "Make America Great Again" sticker on the bumper, and the quip came sliding out before Marc could stop himself. It was intended to be an under-the-breath comment, but the distance between Jake's porch and Christian's driveway wasn't that far, and Marc's normally soft timbre often slipped into a brash stage whisper after a few beers. Jake had shot a sharp glance at Marc, fearing that Christian had heard the quip as he headed toward his own porch with two full bags of groceries.

And now Jake knew that Christian had indeed heard it. At the stove, Christian laughed at Jake's reddening cheeks and gave him another wink. "I personally, like the Captain America comparison best."

"Me, too," said Jake, still blushing.

Christian brought a plate to the table. "And the growing boy gets the first stack." He set the plate in front of Nacho and said, "Don't wait for us, buddy. Dig right in. We'll catch up."

As Nacho dug in with relish, Christian went back to the stove and poured more batter for the next batch. Jake went for the coffee maker, but Christian waved him off.

"Nah, it's all good, I'll get it. Take a seat. These are gonna be ready before you can blink."

Jake took his seat at the table, and sure enough,

practically before he had the chance to blink away the sleep in his eyes, Christian leaned in with a cup of coffee and a fresh plate of fluffy pancakes. For an absurd moment, Jake thought Christian was going to kiss him the way Marc used to when serving him a hot breakfast. But Christian was back at the stove in a flash, pouring batter for the next batch.

"Eat, eat," he called to Jake. "Cold cakes are gross!"

Jake noticed the spread of blueberries, strawberries, and blackberries in bowls on the table, and helped himself, spooning some of each onto his pancakes before pouring syrup over the top. Like everything Christian prepared, it was delicious. Jake thought he could very easily get used to this and had to silently remind himself that Christian's wife, Marilyn, would be returning soon after the house repairs were completed. And shortly after that, Christian would have a child of his own to make breakfasts for.

Christian prepared another plate of pancakes for Nacho before sitting down to his own breakfast. While they ate, he laid out the day's itinerary. With Nacho's help the previous day, they had already managed most of the yard cleanup, leaving only the disposal of the fallen trees. Christian said they could chainsaw the lot and split the spoils for winter firewood. Once the trees were squared away, Christian thought it would be cool to hit the beach for a swim (it was going to be another scorcher today, with temps climbing to over 100°), and Nacho heartily agreed.

Jake was a bit apprehensive and suggested that they leave the fallen trees to a professional yard crew, but Christian and Nacho went straight to work after breakfast.

Jake was pleased when Christian didn't just pull out the chainsaw and start hacking up branches like He-Man in *Masters of the Universe*—or worse, Bruce Campbell in *Ash vs Evil Dead*. He took the time to first cover the safety rules, and Nacho was respectfully observant, asking questions and listening intently.

Christian handled the big logs, and when it came time to cut the smaller ones down to size, he let Nacho have a go with the chainsaw, under his vigilant guidance. Jake stood back and watched his neighbor and the boy, their eyes focused through their protective goggles as they cut the wood. And when the chainsaw was finally retired (much to Jake's relief), all three of them collected and stacked the wood into neat cords along the sides of the two garages.

This didn't take long, and they were off with plenty of sunshine left in the day. Christian made a brief pit-stop on their way to the beach to get a pair of swimming trunks for Nacho at Banana Republic, and Nacho proudly chose the loudest pair he could find, which made Christian laugh with delight because he, too, had a loud pair of trunks.

They had lunch at The Grilled Cheese Hut, a beachfront joint that served hot dogs, burgers, and hoagies in addition to its signature menu item, the best grilled cheese sandwiches on the seven-mile stretch of The Reach that started on the Haven side of the beach and ended just past the western edge of Redemption.

They were finishing their grilled cheeses and washing them down with milkshakes when Christian suggested that they put Jake's huge 4K TV and rockin' sound system to use in the evening with some cool old school flicks. "*The Rock* or *Con Air*," he said, and almost immediately changed his mind. "No. It's a beach day, so we gotta go with the ultimate classic beach day movie. *Point Break!*" Before Jake could voice his opinion, Christian turned to Nacho and said, "Whaddaya say, buddy? You up for some surfer-bank robber action tonight? It's got *Keanu*!"

Jake guessed that Nacho had no clue what *Point Break* was (and the only "Keanu" he might be familiar with was the doorman at The Checkered Skirt), but the boy nodded enthusiastically, as if Christian had suggested another go at the coasters on the Boardwalk or a second run through the cosmic links at The Flamingo. Jake realized with sudden clarity that Nacho's response would have been equally ebullient if Christian had suggested they spend the afternoon painting and then, in the evening, watching the paint dry. The boy would eagerly be up for anything, as long as he got to do it with Christian.

After lunch, they played Frisbee on the beach for a half hour or so before hitting the water. When they took a break, Christian collapsed onto the soft, warm sand with a sigh and a low whistle. "Is there anything this kid can't do? Golfing, pitching, batting—he's a natural! We gotta get him on the disc golf course at the park!"

Jake laughed in agreement. "He's definitely your boy."

"He's *our* boy," Christian corrected. "I can play ball, but he throws that Frisbee like you—ninja-fast and hard as a hammer. Comes in so hot, you almost need a mitt to catch it and a tub of ice water to cool it off. Where'd you learn to throw like that?"

Jake shrugged. "I just always did." He looked out at the shore where Nacho was pitching the Frisbee into the strong southerly wind coming off the water and catching it every time it boomeranged back to him. Jake shook his head with a smile and said, "Of course, I was never as good as *he* is—not at that age, anyway." He smiled, pushing a breath out his nose. "Not at *any* age, actually." He paused as if considering his next words carefully, as if what he was about to say might upset Christian. He took a breath and said with a casual shrug, "So, how old do you think he is? Did we finally fall on a number?"

It was Christian's turn to shrug. "Does it really matter?" And before Jake could respond, Christian was up and running toward the shore, calling, "Go deep, Nach. Hit me."

Nacho threw the disc, nice and long, and Christian caught it at the shoreline. They played for a while until Nacho spied a group of older boys mounting boards and catching waves out on the water.

Christian called out for Nacho to hang tight for a second before heading off to the Baja Hut. Jake watched as Nacho first waited for Christian and then dived into the waves, swimming out as far as he could get until he was tossed back to the shore, laughing with delight.

When Christian returned with a boogie board and jogged out to meet Nacho as he came back into the shore on a small rolling wave, Jake's heart swelled with an unexpected surge of emotion. From his place on the beach towel, he couldn't hear them, but he watched as Christian gave the boy his first surfing lesson. And as with all the other athletic endeavors, Nacho was a natural.

Jake wasn't sure how long they were out on the waves, but by the time they came in and joined him on the shore, the sun was beginning its slow descent on the western horizon. As they toweled off, Christian described some of the cool plot points of *Point Break*, like a kid telling another kid about the kick-ass movie he'd just seen at the cinema, and Nacho listened with rapt attention.

But something was different, Jake thought. Something had changed. He wasn't sure just when this change had taken place, but the dynamic had definitely shifted, and suddenly, Christian and Nacho no longer seemed like brothers goofing around. They seemed like something more. It took Jake a moment to recognize just what that something more was, and when he did, it gave him an odd yet not unpleasant shiver: Christian and Nacho seemed more like a skilled master and a gifted acolyte.

twenty

For dinner, Christian prepared scallops and roasted asparagus on a bed of Asiago lemon risotto, along with crusty sourdough baguettes and Caesar salad. Despite the gourmet meal, which looked like something from a fancy restaurant, they ate at the kitchen table instead of the dining room, where Marc had served special meals. Though Jake had enjoyed Marc's cooking, he'd always found the formal dining room a bit cold. While Christian cooked with Nacho as his sous-chef, Jake set the table in the kitchen, which, by contrast, was warm and cozy, and neither Christian nor Nacho disputed his choice of venue.

While they ate, Nacho asked about the movie again (after hitting the waves at the beach, he was eager to see the surfing bank robbers). Christian told him that it was all taken care of. He'd purchased a 4K digital copy on iTunes for $4.99.

"Talk about a bargain, eh?" he said with a wink. "Now, if you end up enjoying it—and, trust me, you will—you can see it as many times as you like." To Jake, he said, "I sent it to your phone as a gift, so we can download it straight to your hard drive. You do have an account, right?" Jake nodded. "Good because if we download it instead of streaming, there's less of a carbon footprint." Christian grinned. "See? You're turning this Conserva-Sith to the good side of the Force already, Master Jedi. You got me thinking about preserving the planet for this young Padawan." He ruffled Nacho's hair, and the boy smiled.

Jake smiled, too, but his eyes looked distant, as if they weren't in on the act. He hoped Christian and Nacho didn't notice, but he couldn't help himself. It wasn't anything Christian had said, but rather the *way* he'd said it. Or to a finer point, the way he'd effortlessly translated what he was saying into ASL without being consciously aware that he was using both his mouth and his hands to communicate.

It was nine o'clock by the time they finished dinner and got the kitchen squared away. And it was half past nine by the time they got themselves situated on the sofa in front of Jake's huge screen, with a big bowl of popcorn and drinks. Nacho sat between Jake and Christian, but as the movie progressed, Jake noticed the boy inching closer to Christian, especially during the more intense scenes.

At first, Jake had been a little worried that, after the long day, Nacho might doze off before the movie was over. But Nacho remained wide awake, from the opening titles to the end of the credit crawl. Jake, who didn't have any younger siblings and had never experienced a thrilling movie through the eyes of another kid, found himself paying nearly as much attention to Nacho as he did to the movie itself. The kid was positively enamored with all the

action. Christian was riveted to the screen as well, but Jake
noticed his occasional glances at the boy throughout to
gauge his reaction.

Jake was struck by the gravely solemn expressions
on both Christian and Nacho's faces as Bodhi, the head
surfer-bank robber, headed into the waves at Bells Beach,
Australia, in the big finale. Jake didn't consider himself a
cynical guy, but he expected he might have laughed or at
least smiled at Marc having the same reaction to this scene.

But it was different with Christian and Nacho. Jake
didn't feel like smiling or laughing at them, because neither was like Marc, who could cry buckets at a sad movie
and then two minutes after it was over, slip between the
sheets with Jake as if they'd just watched a steamy sex romp
instead of a heartbreaking tear-jerker. Because, to Marc, it
was just a movie, filled with disposable emotion and over-
paid actors moving around sound stages like puppets on
strings while cameras recorded the fabrication.

It was not, however, "just a movie" to Christian and
Nacho. For them, it was a rite of passage.

The movie ended shortly after eleven-thirty, but after
brushing his teeth and climbing into bed, Nacho was still
far too wired from the experience to fall straight to sleep.
He sat up under the covers in Jake's guest room, discussing his favorite parts of the movie with Christian, his face
bright as his hands moved in big, sweeping gestures to
Christian's delight.

Down in the kitchen, Jake finished with the cleanup and
started the dishwasher before heading upstairs. He didn't
enter the room. He stood in the hallway just outside the
open door, listening to Christian's end of the conversation

and extrapolating Nacho's end from Christian's laughter and responses. He remained there, with his eyes closed and his back against the wall next to the open door, and only after it became silent inside did he open his eyes and look into the room.

Moonlight spilled through the window, illuminating the two figures in silhouette: Christian sitting on the edge of the bed, Nacho tucked under the covers, both of them signing.

Christian: *It's late. Time to go to sleep, buddy.*

Nacho: *Just a bit longer. Please.*

Christian: *We've still got a lot of work to do tomorrow. I need you up bright and early. Jake's a lazy head. I need you to help me motivate him.*

Nacho smiled at this. He knew Christian was only kidding about Jake being a lazy head. But then something strange happened. The boy hesitated a moment and then signed something that sent a wave of gooseflesh racing over Jake's body: *Just stay until I fall asleep. He won't come and get me if you're here.*

As chilling as that statement was, Christian didn't react with alarm. He responded calmly and rationally, as a parent would upon hearing their child voice concern over a monster in the closet or under the bed. And just as he'd done at the dinner table, he spoke with both his voice and his hands. "No one is coming to get you, buddy. I'll make sure of it."

Nacho signed, *You promise?*

Christian signed, *I promise.*

He brushed the hair back from Nacho's brow and kissed him gently on the forehead.

When the boy curled up into his pillow, he looked small and vulnerable. Jake noticed that he was hugging the stuffed elephant that Christian had won for him at the shooting gallery, and automatically, he reached for the friendship bracelet that Nacho had won for him at the bottle toss. He stroked the woven embroidery floss bracelet with his fingertips, comforted to find it was still there where Christian had secured it with a permanent knot (Nacho had been adamant about the knot being permanent because a friendship bracelet was permanent and should never be removed).

Jake stepped silently away from the door and went back downstairs.

Christian appeared in the kitchen archway a half hour later and said, "All good. He's off to sleep, like a baby." He smiled—or at least it looked like a smile; in the shadowy kitchen, it was hard to tell. "That was a good day," he said, his voice sounding a little thick, like maybe he was coming down with a cold or something. Then his voice sounded normal again. "I think we should let him sleep in tomorrow. There really isn't much more cleanup to do. Maybe we'll make it another beach day or hit the Museum Campus. I think he'd love the aquarium."

Christian's eyes shone briefly in the darkness, and he swiped at them with the heels of his hands. He did this with a yawn that Jake thought may or may not have been genuine.

"Man, am I tired!" he said, with a laugh that was a little more convincing than the yawn. "I'm gonna get out of your hair and hit the sack. G'night."

Jake stood in the dark for a long time after the door in

the foyer closed behind Christian. He stood very quietly, as if listening for the sound of a closet door opening in the room above . . . or hands and legs crawling out from under a bed up there.

Just stay until I fall asleep. He won't come and get me if you're here.

Jake closed his eyes and recalled an image from his swimming days: the large stop-clock on the painted brick wall opposite the diving blocks . . . only, in his imagination, the clock wasn't hanging on the wall of the high school natatorium. It was floating in the darkness above his bed, ticking away seconds, inching closer to zero.

Christian had entrusted him with the boy's safety, and Jake was ready to bolt for the stairs at the first sound of a creaking hinge or floorboard. It was too soon, and Christian wasn't prepared to let go yet.

But no one came for the boy that night.

twenty-one

O n the morning of the sixth day after the storm, Jake woke from a dream that was already fading by the time his feet touched the carpet. He sat on the edge of the bed, rubbing sleep from his eyes as he tried to remember the details, but the only one he could grasp with any clarity was the location of the dream. He had been back in the wheat field at sunrise, barefoot and shirtless. But everything else was a blur.

He went to the bathroom to take care of his morning business, and only after he'd come back into the room did he realize there was no aroma of hot breakfast wafting up from the kitchen. He padded down the hall to the guest room, expecting to find Nacho still asleep—it was early, and Christian had said to let him sleep in. But the boy wasn't there, and the bed was neatly made. This woke him fully, and he headed down the stairwell with more than a measure of urgency.

The kitchen was empty. The table wasn't even set with

bowls and glasses for cold cereal and orange juice. The coffee maker was silent, too. Jake's heart seemed to skip a beat as a wave of panic swept through him. He raced to the living room, and what he found there made him stop dead in the archway.

"Morning, sleepy head," Christian said with a smile. "I didn't want to wake you before I had this guy up and dressed. Go ahead, hit the shower and suit up, Nightwing. Captain America and Blue Beetle here will watch cartoons until you're ready." He tickled Nacho's tummy, and the boy laughed.

Jake gazed into the living room, scarcely able to credit his own eyes. Nacho was dressed in new clothing, presumably from the bag on the floor at the end of the coffee table. The bag featured a black-and-white image of three boys tumbling on the grass; the logo read: *"abercrombie kids"* in all lowercase letters.

But this wasn't what had halted Jake in his tracks.

It was the boy's appearance that had done that. The change, this time, was unmistakable. And undeniable. He could no longer pass for thirteen. Nor twelve or eleven, or even ten or nine. Nacho was no more than seven or eight.

Jake tried to rationalize the transformation in his mind—just as he had done with all the other changes in the boy's appearance over the past few days.

But this was too stark for rationalizations. The boy they first met outside of The Checkered Skirt had been an eighteen-year-old young man. Jake was absolutely sure of this. And somehow, over the course of four days, that young man had regressed at least ten years, and was now a seven- or eight-year-old child.

Jake was still frozen in the entryway between the hall and the living room when Christian chuckled softly, "I guess my mom was right. It's like you need to buy all new clothes within days of the last set you bought. Come on, man, chop-chop. We have to go for breakfast before we hit the Museum Campus. Go get cleaned up."

Jake was still frozen, looking at Nacho, who smiled and signed, "Chop-chop."

Jake turned and went back upstairs, almost like a somnambulist. He brushed his teeth and showered by rote while his mind remained focused on what had just happened down in his living room—or rather, what *hadn't* happened.

Christian had acted as if nothing out of the ordinary was going on, as if it were any other day. And in a way, Jake supposed it *was* like any other day—at least for Christian, it was. Aside from buying new clothes and shoes for the boy when the old ones had become visibly too loose, Christian hadn't reacted at all to the changes in Nacho's physical appearance over the past four days. Jake could hardly fault him for this. Who would believe something so utterly out there could be happening in real life? It was the stuff of pure fantasy, where a kid can drop a coin into a Zoltar machine and wish to become big overnight . . . or a guy can be born old and de-age throughout his life before dying as an infant in his cradle.

But with the irrefutable evidence of that fantasy-turned-factual sitting right there on the sofa in front of him, how could Christian ignore it? How could he willfully bury his head in the sand and pretend it wasn't happening?

For a crazy half-second, Jake actually entertained his

own bit of rationalizing, imagining a wild scenario in which Christian had masterminded this whole thing, hired the young woman and a group of brothers, ages eighteen through eight, all of them identical, of course, so they could step in, virtually undetected, as the "plot" advanced daily. Exactly *why* Christian would do this was beyond Jake, but at least it would be more credible than what was clearly happening.

Jake dressed and went downstairs, where he stood in the archway between the hall and the living room, watching Christian and Nacho. The boy was on Christian's lap, leaning back against his chest as they watched *Super Kitties* on Disney Jr. The Super Kitties were singing a song, and Jake couldn't help studying the boy in Christian's arms, looking for some telltale sign that he was not, in fact, the teenager they had taken in three nights ago—a mole, a scar, a variation in the color of his eyes, anything that would explain the inexplicable.

But there was nothing out of place. The boy was unmistakably Nacho—the tumble of messy hair, the long, dark eyelashes, the crooked dimples, the sweetly blunted nose, the intensely focused set of his eyes, one slightly darker than the other.

Jake listened to the song, and his heart skipped a beat when, without taking his eyes from the TV screen, Nacho reached up and touched Christian's cheek with his fingertips as the kitties sang:

> *And when we're takin' a break*
> *From the hero work we do,*
> *It's still the best day ever*
> *'Cause I'm spendin' it with you . . .*

Jake waited until the final line of the song—"*Best day ever*"—echoed off before stepping back into the hall and calling out to the living room, "You guys ready?"

twenty-two

They had breakfast at Silvia's, a cozy pancake house in Redemption's historic downtown district. They were served by Silvia herself, a small Puerto Rican woman with a lush head of curly hair and beautiful brown eyes that lit up whenever she smiled, which she did often. They all had Belgian waffles. Silvia brought their order, and Nacho smiled bashfully when she set his plate in front of him and said in Spanish, "For the handsomest boy I've ever had the pleasure of serving." To Nacho's delight, his waffle was adorned with a curved line of fresh blueberries placed in the shape of a smiling mouth, two small strawberries for the eyes, and a pat of butter for the nose.

After breakfast, they headed straight for Museum Campus on the Point. It was a bright, sunny day, but with the northerly breeze off the lake, the temperature felt a good 15° cooler than it had been in the driveway back home, making it a comfortable 77°.

They went to the Museum of Natural History first. Nacho marveled at the massive pillars and ornate façade out front. His eyes grew even wider when they entered the building. The dinosaur display was up and running, and the lights were set appropriately low, with green, red, purple, yellow, and blue floodlights illuminating the various sections. The creatures all looked so realistic that Nacho took both Christian and Jake's hands and remained between them throughout the tour, which stretched well beyond the grand hall, into equally atmospherically lit chambers, where all manner of dinosaurs crouched behind shrubs and trees, as if waiting to pounce. There were cool sound effects, too, which added nicely to the experience.

Christian chuckled, pitching his voice low to Jake: "Things have certainly changed since we were kids, eh? Back then, a day at the museum was like a real snooze fest. All they had was a bunch of bones propped up on pedestals. This is like Jurassic Park in here!" He squeezed Nacho's hand reassuringly and smiled down at him. "You OK, buddy? You want to keep going?"

Nacho nodded, his eyes alight with a mixture of trepidation and anticipation. He wanted to keep going.

Christian smiled a soft smile at Jake and gave the boy's hand another gentle squeeze. "OK. But I think Jake's a little apprehensive here. I think you'll need to hold onto his hand a little tighter and help him through this one, y'know?"

Nacho squeezed Jake's hand tighter, and Jake squeezed back reassuringly, struck by how small the boy's hand felt in his own.

The sign at the entrance said the dino tour usually took a little over an hour to complete, but since there was no guide and no strict timetable, they took it a little slower at the parts Nacho liked best, and ended up exiting the exhibit shortly after noon.

They had a light lunch on the lakeside terrace out-side the museum. Nacho and Jake had veggie wraps, but Christian was unable to resist the aroma of the beef hot dogs coming from a nearby vendor's cart.

"I've been eating healthy all week—save for those 'Dunkin' detours,' but they don't really count, because we worked off all those calories on the lawn cleanup." Taking a big bite out of his loaded pup, Christian dropped a wink and grin, adding, "So I'm entitled to a little cheat."

After lunch, they hit the planetarium, where they lay back in their seats, with Nacho between them, gazing breathlessly at the history of the universe projected onto the massive domed screen.

After the show, they explored the exhibits. Nacho's favorite was the Hall of Maps, which, to his complete sur-prise and utter delight, didn't contain maps at all! Indeed, it was a dimly lit chamber, where three-dimensional holo-graphic images of the universe hovered, bringing planets, moons, supernovas, and even asteroids within touching distance. Nacho liked how you could stroll the floor and move about the holograms to view them from different angles. He stayed in this room for nearly an hour, trans-fixed by all the sights, and would have stayed even longer if Christian hadn't reminded him that they still had the aquarium to visit.

As Christian had predicted, the boy fell in love with the aquarium, especially the glass-tunneled corridors, where every manner of fish and sea creature could be seen swimming so close that, if not for the protective glass, you could have reached out and touched them. He adored the dolphins and the schools of colorful fish that bulleted by at lightning speed. And he found the sharks that swam through a separate glass tunnel of their own fascinating.

But his favorite occupants of the aquarium were, by far, the otters in the Horn Oceanarium, a large naturalistic environment, conducive to their species. Nacho was enraptured by the playful creatures, who seemed more than happy to perform for him. One otter in particular tirelessly entertained the boy with dives from the ledge and deep, spiraling plunges into the water.

"That's Ein," said a young woman in a pink Horn Oceanarium T-shirt. "He's begging for treats and won't stop until he gets some." With a look at her watch, she added, "And it's almost time. Would you like to give him a few?"

Nacho's eyes lit up. Christian smiled, ruffling the boy's hair. But Jake looked a little apprehensive.

"He'll be perfectly safe," the woman said. "Ein's our best boy and a complete show-off. He loves attention and treats." To Nacho, she said, "Come on, sweetie. I'll take you to the platform."

They followed the woman through the gate and up the steps to the platform, where Ein the otter was already waiting.

"I'm Krystal," the woman said when they reached the top.

Christian introduced them all—by their real names this time. He stopped and raised an eyebrow at Nacho, as if to make sure that Nacho's name change hadn't gone into effect yet. The boy nodded and signed, "Not yet."

Krystal gave Christian a curious smile.

"He's not sure he likes his nickname anymore, and he's considering changing it."

J. T. Holden

Krystal said, "What's wrong with Nacho? That's a pretty cool nickname."

Nacho held his hand out flat, wavered it from side to side, and signed, "For now."

Krystal laughed sweetly and signed back, "Well, just make sure you pick a good one."

Nacho nodded. Jake looked at Krystal curiously.

Krystal laughed that sweet laugh again. "I took ASL in college." She signed this for Nacho, who nodded and smiled.

Jake didn't bother telling her that Nacho wasn't deaf, that he just didn't speak. And it didn't matter because Nacho was already on the platform with Krystal, feeding treats to Ein, the otter.

When another otter swam up to the platform, Nacho's eyes lit up again, and Krystal said, "That's Flirt. She's the only one who can horn in on Ein's treat time." She lowered her voice to a conspiratorial whisper and winked. "Ein's sweet on her, and lets her get away with anything." She crossed her fingers. "We're hoping that Flirt and Ein will get together and bring us some pups soon. Their breed is endangered."

Nacho's eyes shone gravely, and for a moment, Jake thought tears might bloom, but the boy remained strong. And after Flirt took a handful of berries from his outstretched palm, Ein came in and pushed his head into Nacho's empty hand, and the boy smiled as he petted the otter's head.

Flirt came back to do the same, and Nacho petted her, too. When Ein shook his head, a spray of water dappled Nacho's face, and he laughed. After more treats and petting for both otters, the couple swam off, swirling about each other and nudging heads.

Krystal laughed, "I think you might have brought them together with all the treats and petting. Let's hope they make good parents."

It was half past seven when they left the aquarium. They had dinner at a quaint Italian restaurant on the wharf and then walked off the calories on the pier afterward. Nacho made it on foot all the way out to the lighthouse, where he gazed out at the moonlit water with the wonder of a child experiencing something for the very first time. But on the way back, he got tired, and Christian hoisted him up into one arm and carried him the rest of the way.

By the time they reached the car, the boy was asleep, with his head resting on Christian's shoulder. Christian fished his keys out of his pocket and pitched them to Jake. "You drive. I'll sit in back with him."

Jake took the keys and got behind the wheel of Christian's Jeep. He didn't have to adjust anything; he and Christian were roughly the same height. He looked into the rear-view mirror a few times on the way home, but all he could make out was the silhouette of Christian with the boy still asleep in his arms.

It wasn't until he brought the Jeep to a stop in the driveway and got out that he noticed the change. Nacho's new clothes, which had fit him perfectly that morning, now hung loose, like hand-me-downs from a child at least two years older than he. Jake's lips parted, but Christian was already headed up the path to Jake's front door with the sleeping boy in his arms.

Jake stood in the foyer, waiting for Christian to come

back down after putting Nacho to bed. They needed to talk. But when Christian didn't return after ten minutes, Jake headed up the stairs.

He expected to find Christian tucking the boy into the guest room bed. Instead, he found them in the master bedroom at the far end of the hall.

Nacho was asleep under the covers. He was in the same spot he'd occupied three nights ago when they'd had their first sleepover, but looking infinitely smaller. Christian stood gazing down at him. The look in Christian's eyes almost halted Jake. But then he gathered up his courage and spoke. "I think we need to discuss—"

But that was as far as he could get.

"We had a good day," Christian cut in softly. "Please don't spoil it."

Jake looked down at his shoes. He didn't want to see the look in Christian's eyes if the guy chose to hit him with a shot of those steely blues; he didn't think he could take the intensity of such an assault just now.

Christian sighed almost soundlessly. "Let's just go to bed, and we'll deal with it in the morning. OK?"

Jake said softly, "OK."

Without another word, Christian went to the bathroom, and when he returned, he was clad only in his boxers and T-shirt. He climbed into his side of the bed while Jake shut out the light and went to the bathroom.

When Jake returned a few minutes later, he climbed into bed on the other side of Nacho, listening for Christian's breathing to fall in with the steady rhythm set by the slumbering boy between them.

It didn't come for a long time. And by the time it finally

did, Jake had already drifted off to sleep. In retrospect, he would think, *If only one of us had been able to stay awake till morning.* But in his heart, he knew that nothing would have changed the outcome.

Even before they'd met the boy, it was already too late.

twenty-three

Jake's dream of the wheat field came again shortly before the sun rose on the morning of the seventh day after the storm. And this time, Jake remembered all of it when he opened his eyes.

He didn't roll over; he didn't need to. He knew without looking that he was alone in the bed that was far too big for just one person—and further, that something had been taken from him during the hours he'd slept, something that could not be replaced. He also knew that the wheat field dream wasn't just a recurring dream; it was a *progressive* one.

He sighed soundlessly as he replayed the final installment of the dream like a movie in his mind, concentrating on the new "footage."

The white wolf was back and racing through the wheat maze, but he was no longer alone. This time, he was followed by a smaller wolf, mirroring his every move with the clumsy alacrity of a vibrant young pup.

Jake stood as before, barefoot and shirtless, watching

as the two wolves, the large white one and the dark pup, chased the voles out of the wheat maze. The cat was there, too, herding the younger wolf when he got distracted by the dragonflies, of which there were many, soaring above the tall shoots of wheat like dive bombers gunning for the voles. When the pup fell out of step with the alpha, the cat bounded in for a course-correction and then immediately rejoined the large white wolf to drive out the voles.

After the field was clear of all intruders, the white wolf and the dark pup tussled playfully in the wheat. And no matter how many times the pup climbed onto his back and chewed on his ears, the alpha never became agitated, never snapped or snarled. And Jake understood intuitively that the white wolf would never leave the pup, never tire of him, never push him away. They were bonded now, and the white wolf would always be there for the pup. He would raise him and defend him and keep him warm and safe.

Though the two wolves were clearly familial, they shared only one distinguishing feature: identical markings on the inside of their front left legs, like a brand or a birthmark (Jake noticed this as they wrestled). Otherwise, the dark pup looked like . . .

The dream shifted focus—back to Jake as he stood gazing out at the two wolves indecisively. The pup stopped wrestling and looked up sharply, ears pricked at a sudden sound from the wheat. The pup waited, and momentarily his patience was rewarded.

Out of the tall shoots of wheat, a familiar object rolled. Jake recognized it at once—it had been the center of his universe throughout his youth, from his first day in grammar school when a group of boys invited him to join them on the pitch to his last game in high school when he hammered in the winning goal to take his team to the nationals (which, unfortunately, he didn't get to attend, due to the injury he sustained while hammering in said goal).

The soccer ball rolled straight past the pup and stopped under Jake's foot. The pup sat up eagerly, and Jake smiled knowingly. Standing with his planting foot next to the ball, toes aimed straight at the mouth of the maze, Jake drew back, locking the ankle of his kicking foot, and took the shot. He nailed it perfectly with the top of his foot—right where the laces of his shoe would have been were he not barefoot.

The ball soared low into the maze, and the pup bolted after it, with the alpha in pursuit. And still Jake stood, tentative, teetering on the edge between the world he knew and the one he yearned to explore. He wanted to run with the wolves, but wasn't sure he could transform into such a magnificent and uninhibited creature. Not yet, anyway.

The dream had ended with Jake still on the precipice, not knowing if he was capable of taking the plunge into the wheat maze.

When he finally got out of bed, Jake took a longer-than-usual shower. Despite the aroma of coffee, scrambled eggs, and fresh cinnamon rolls wafting up the stairwell, he was in no hurry to get down to the kitchen this morning.

He wasn't surprised to find Christian setting two plates on the table. But he *was* surprised at Christian's greeting as he came down the stairs, pulling on his T-shirt.

"Morning, sleepyhead. I thought this would wake you. Sorry the rolls are only the store-bought kind. I always make them from scratch. I should've made them from scratch for—" He shook his head. "I'll do them for you sometime. You'll love 'em. We can gorge until we're bloated and then swim off all the calories at the beach. Or maybe go mountain biking. You have a bike, don't you? Didn't I see you biking with that Marc guy once? Or we can go surfing. You've got the perfect build for boarding—I still have to teach you proper practice paddling and pop-ups. We sort of just skimmed over that stuff last time and got straight to the waves."

Only that's not exactly what Christian said. What he actually said was, "*He's* got the perfect build for board-ing—I still have to teach *him* proper practice-paddling and pop-ups . . . "

But Christian showed no sign that he'd misspoken. He just loaded scrambled eggs onto their plates, chuckling ironically, "I can't believe I used to love bacon and sausage with eggs, and now the thought of either makes me want to hurl. What was I thinking, having that hot dog yesterday? *That* didn't settle well." He chuckled again, with a sigh. "I must be growing up, ready for some responsibility. Out of the mouths of babes, am I right?"

Jake nodded, but he gazed at Christian as one might a person who's not operating on all cylinders.

"Eat, eat," Christian said, unaware of Jake's gaze. "We've got a full day ahead of us, and you'll need to be operating on all cylinders if you're gonna keep up with Captain America. I think we can salvage most of those loose siding panels. And we can order replacements for the ones that are too far gone."

They worked throughout the long, hot morning, and when the sun piqued at midday, Jake didn't need an invi-tation to peel off his shirt. He just followed suit when Christian took off his own and pitched it onto the porch. He smiled when Christian whistled and quipped with a grin,

"You know we're gonna end up in the shower together by the end of this day, right?"

When Jake shot back with a grin, "Yeah, right. You couldn't handle this action, straight boy," Christian didn't laugh his usual high-pitched laugh. Instead, he just kept on fitting the siding panels into place as he made his response almost under his breath.

"You'd be surprised what this 'straight boy' can handle."

Jake smiled, handing another siding panel up to Christian on the ladder. He knew they were only joking, but it heartened him to see Christian ribbing him like his old self again. He didn't believe this sudden segway into humor meant that Christian was over what had happened, not by a long shot. And he understood that, eventually, they would have to have a serious discussion about the strange events of the past week. Who else could either of them talk to about it without risking being thrown into the local loony bin for a serious psych evaluation and years of intensive therapy sessions with a battery of shrinks?

Still, Christian's ability to joke and tease was a good sign. Jake thought that being out in the sunshine and working with his hands like this was the best thing for him. For both of them, actually.

They took a quick lunch break around one and then resumed work until the sun began its descent in the west. They'd gotten the loose siding back up on both houses, and even fixed the fascia on Christian's house (remarkably, Jake's had escaped the storm's wrath unscathed). They had decided on Chinese takeaway for dinner, and both went into their separate houses at seven to wash up.

Jake was upstairs and ready to hop into the shower when something Christian had said at lunch came back to him. Christian was looking up at the repairs with an unreadable expression. Then, he looked down at his sandwich that he really didn't want to eat and said softly, "Doesn't matter if the whole thing goes to shit. What's the point if you're not gonna be there to enjoy it?"

It didn't register for Jake at the time. They were just shooting the breeze and eating deli sandwiches that Jake didn't have the appetite for either.

But now, for some reason, the statement leapt out at him.

What's the point if you're not gonna be there to enjoy it?

Jake was already half-naked when this memory occurred, and quickly pulled his clothes back on as he headed for the stairs.

Christian's front door wasn't open, but it was unlocked, and Jake took the stairs two at a time. He expected the sound of water from the bathroom to greet him, but there was only silence at the top of the stairs.

He didn't head to the open door of the master bedroom at the end of the short hall. He found Christian kneeling before the crib in the shadow-streaked nursery, with his back to the open door.

Jake stood very still for a moment. He was about to say something—just what, he didn't know—when Christian's voice came softly but clearly from the shadows. "I didn't send her away . . . "

At first, Jake thought he'd misheard and was about to ask for clarification when Christian's voice came again.

"My wife," Christian said, still gazing into the crib.

"I didn't send her away because of the storm." He paused briefly before continuing in that same soft tone. "I didn't send her away for her and the baby's safety, because there isn't going to be a baby." Another beat. "At least that's what Mare told me. When I asked her doctor, he said he couldn't 'speak to the specifics'. All he could tell me was that my wife was no longer pregnant. I asked him what that meant, and he said I would have to speak to my wife about it." Christian made a slight sound in his throat, and Jake remained silent. Then Christian said, "I didn't ask her. I couldn't, because if she could do something like that—" He swallowed softly, his eyes moist and distant. "I didn't want to know it. I didn't want to think of her that way, you know? I couldn't think of her that way. Not that way."

Jake stood silent, but his temples throbbed with the slow, driving beat of his heart. For a second, it felt as if he were free-falling down an endless dark hole. Then, he was pulled back by the sound of Christian clearing his throat.

"After she lost the baby, she said she was leaving to stay with her sister in Arizona. She said it would be best if we didn't talk for a while, so she could figure things out. So, I helped her pack and put her things in her car."

Jake remembered seeing Christian and Marilyn in their driveway about a week before the storm had hit. After Christian had loaded her bags into the trunk of the white Lexus, the two had embraced for a long time. Jake remembered that Marilyn had let go first, leaving Christian to tuck his hands into the pockets of his cargo shorts and stand there awkwardly as she backed out of the driveway and drove off. Jake remembered thinking how Captain America: The First Avenger suddenly looked more like Spider-Man:

Far from Home—still stacked with fully loaded guns and abs you could wash laundry on, but reduced and infinitely younger, like a teenage boy dumped on prom night. And Jake remembered one other detail: Christian and his beautiful wife had not exchanged a goodbye kiss.

Jake still didn't know if he should speak or what he would say if he dared to chime in.

It didn't matter because Christian wasn't finished.

"She said it was probably for the best . . . you know, her losing the . . . " He stopped and cleared his throat softly again before continuing. "Because the baby would have made things . . . difficult for us . . . to separate when I . . . eventually . . . " He let it trail off.

Jake stood silent in the doorway, blood crashing at his temples in near-dizzying waves now.

"I would have made it work," Christian said, his voice softer still. "I *could* have made it work for the baby. She knew that I would have done anything to make it work for the baby. I have willpower, and I would have made a great dad . . . the best dad . . . a fierce dad. I would have protected him with my life."

The young woman spoke suddenly and urgently inside Jake's head: *You must trust the white wolf—is only one who can protect boy when kotchka is off running.*

A wave of tendrils crawled Jake's spine as the woman's warning echoed in his mind.

Then the silence was broken again.

"I don't think it was a miscarriage," Christian said in that impossibly soft voice. "And I don't know how she could do that." There was no rancor in him; he didn't even look angry. He looked like a boy, lost and teetering on the verge of a breakdown. "I know I'm a dick and I wouldn't have been a very good husband . . . but I would have been a good dad." He paused. "We *both* would have."

A single tear rolled down his cheek, and despite the heat in the room, Jake shivered.

"He was *ours*," Christian seethed with sudden fierceness (*Like a wolf,* Jake thought). "He came to *us*, and he was *ours*." He pressed his forehead to the railing of the crib. Another tear fell, but he didn't cry. "I will give you my life if you just bring him back to us. I swear it."

The chill struck again, causing Jake's body to race with gooseflesh, when Christian reached into the shadows under the crib and took something out. And this time, Jake couldn't stop himself.

"Don't," he said in a soft yet commanding whisper.

Christian turned, startled, with the object he'd retrieved from under the crib in his hand. Jake flinched, reflexively raising his hands in a useless defensive gesture to ward off the shot. But no gunshot rang out because the object Christian held in his hand was just the prize Christian had won for Nacho on Gallery Row.

"Jesus, fuck, dude!" Christian spat, expelling a shaky breath. "Don't *do* that!"

"I thought you were—"

"What?" Christian snapped.

"I thought you were gonna—" He halted at Christian's steely blue gaze, and swallowed. "It looked like a gun."

Christian looked at the stuffed animal in his trembling hand. "What?" He laughed without humor. "You thought I was gonna kill myself with this?" He shook his head and expelled another shaky breath. "You just gave me a jolt. I didn't know you were there."

"You were talking to me," Jake said, confused.

"Yeah, Christian said. "But I didn't know you were *actually* there." On Jake's continued confusion, Christian snapped, "You've never talked to somebody who wasn't there that you wished was there?"

Jake's lips parted, but he didn't know how to respond.

Christian looked down at the stuffed elephant in his hand, and his anger evaporated in a soundless sigh. After a moment, he said, "He didn't choose this one for the baby. He knew that there wasn't going to be a baby because the baby was already . . . "

He stopped, and his nostrils flared briefly, but again, he didn't cry. Jake remained silent.

"Don't ask me how he knew it. He just knew it. Like he knew which cabinet you keep the glasses in at your place and where to find your stash of fig bars. Or how to flip that switch to turn on the filtered water on your faucet in the kitchen sink. He just knew things. Like he knew that I was gonna slip on the roof and caught me before I could fall off and break my stupid neck. And if you don't believe that, I really don't give a shit. I know what I know, and I believe what I believe. There are things in this universe that people don't always have the answers for 'em, you know." He sighed softly through his nose. "Sometimes, when things don't make sense, you just have to have faith."

Jake nodded, but he wasn't sure if this was because he believed in what Christian had just said or because he didn't want to upset him any more than he already was.

Christian sighed again, still looking at the stuffed elephant. He stroked a thumb over its soft fur. "And he didn't choose it for some bullshit political reason. He chose it because elephants represent wisdom, strength, loyalty, patience, and family. And if you're gonna smirk at that, you can turn around and walk out right now because you're clearly not the person I thought you were, and I don't need that kind of snarky shit in my life."

But Jake didn't smirk. And he didn't turn and walk out. Instead, he reached out and put a hand on Christian's shoulder. He didn't know how he'd gotten from the door to the crib—he didn't even remember stepping into the room. All he knew was that he was at Christian's side in solidarity. And when he finally spoke, he did so without parting his lips.

And his silent words surprised him.

I don't know if I have faith—at least not the kind you have. But I know I don't want to be alone tonight . . . and I need to know if you want the same thing.

He waited for Christian's response, which came in a single gentle nod.

twenty-four

When they reached the top of the stairs at Jake's house, he assumed that Christian would head straight for the guest bathroom, and after they were showered and dressed, they would pick up the Chinese takeaway, or maybe they would dine in at the restaurant. But Christian only stopped to place the bundle of his fresh clothes on the vanity in the guest bath before following Jake to the master bedroom at the end of the hall.

Jake wasn't aware that Christian had followed him until after he'd turned on the taps in the master bath and ducked under the showerhead. He was lathering up when the glass door opened behind him, and Christian stepped into the stall, naked.

For a moment, they stood under the warm stream from the showerhead, like figures in a tableau, neither sure of what to do next. Christian made the first move. It was clumsy but gentle, and Jake allowed him to explore without comment or criticism. He had been used to Marc's aggressive approach, and hadn't been prepared for the tender, almost tentative probing of Christian's hands, which trembled disarmingly.

Christian chuckled softly, nervously, and spoke in a near-whisper, "I don't know if I'm doing this right . . . maybe you could show me . . . and I could—"

Before he could finish, Jake wrapped a tender hand around the back of his neck and kissed him, and the nervous trembling instantly gave way to another sensation, one that made Christian feel infinitely calmer as he willingly ceded control to Jake. And as the two of them fell into a unified rhythm that Christian had never achieved with anyone before, including the handful of times he'd experimented with other guys in high school, everything became clear for him.

It was the same for Jake, who couldn't help recalling his ex's sly assertion as they'd said their goodbyes on the porch that last day . . .

He's probably a real power-bottom. Perfect for you. Capitulation with strength. Just your speed.

But it was more than just that, Jake thought afterward. When the lovemaking was done, Christian didn't nip down the hall to take a private shower in the guest bath as Marc had always done after what he jokingly referred to as "a little water sports," usually adding with a wink, *It's too crowded in here for the both of us to wash up at the same time. We'll just keep knocking cocks, and I'll end up wanting to fuck you all over again.*

Christian had stayed in the shower with Jake to wash up. And the look in his eyes was different than Marc's. Though bashful and still slightly timid, his eyes didn't look like they were elsewhere. He didn't look like Marc often did after sex, like the entire experience had been nothing more than a business transaction, like it was pointless—even silly—for the two of them to still be naked when it was time to move on to the next deal.

Unlike Marc, Christian was comfortable being naked with Jake after the "deal was done." He took the bar of soap and washed Jake's back and shoulders. And when he was done, he gave the bar to Jake and asked him to do the same for him, and Jake did. And when they turned off the taps and stepped from the shower, Christian did something that Marc had never done.

He leaned in while they were toweling off and kissed Jake on the lips. There was no tongue or intimation that he was ready for another go. It was a sweet and gentle kiss that made Jake wish they could crawl straight into bed. He suspected that Christian would be a great after-sex cuddler, and he would have liked nothing better than to fall asleep in his arms after the long and revealing day they had shared.

Christian grinned with that short, high-pitched laugh that Jake had grown to love, and as if reading Jake's mind, he said, "We can cuddle later—scratch that. We *will* cuddle later. But right now, I'm fuckin' starving. Are we still going for Chinese?"

They did go for Chinese, but they didn't bring it home. Instead, they ate at the restaurant and stopped off at The Checkered Skirt for a beer afterward. When they sat down at one of the patio tables, a familiar voice called out, "Saxon and Lochy! I thought we lost you guys for a minute there!"

Keanu came to their table with a big smile, and he and

Christian exchanged the mystifying handshake of young demigods that Jake was pretty sure he himself would never be able to master. But this didn't stop Keanu from giving it a go with him. Jake didn't fare too well at the handshake, but Keanu laughed good-naturedly.

"No worries, bro. We'll work on it. Pretty soon, you'll be as good as Saxon here."

"Yeah, about that," Christian said with a glance at Jake that said he was going to restart and proceed on a no bull-shit plank from here on out. He told Keanu their real names and apologized for using the fake ones. "We were incognito when we first met you and weren't sure where things were going yet."

Keanu smiled like it was all good and said that he'd figured as much. With a wink, he added, "I mean, what are the odds that a couple of hot guys named Saxon and Lochy would sit down at my station on the night of a full moon? *The White Lotus* is one of my faves, bro . . . especially the Full Moon Party where Lochy gives Saxon that hand job."

Christian laughed, and he and Keanu looked directly at Jake before quoting in unison: "'Lochy, it's OK for you to like worship me, but don't like . . .'" They thrust their hands at their crotches before delivering the final line in strained whispers: "'. . . *worship* me!'"

And then, they both burst into gales of laughter. Jake smiled, like someone who doesn't get the joke but is happy to see others happy. Keanu said, "Have you seen it?"

Jake shook his head, and Christian nearly spilled his beer with wide eyes. "Oh my God, you haven't seen *The White Lotus*? What fuckin' planet have you been living on? You've *got* to see it! You got HBO next door?" Jake shook his head. Christian waved it off, sipping his beer. "No sweat. I'll put you on my plan. We're definitely watching it, and we gotta do it on that sweet set of yours next door."

Keanu raised a brow. "You guys don't live together?"

Christian looked at Jake, took a breath, and held it before expelling it in a slow stream. With a slightly sheepish grin, he said, "We're working on that one."

Keanu smiled. "Well, at least you got the pre-engagement out of the way." On Christian's curious smile, Keanu nodded at the friendship bracelet on his wrist. "The Kumihimo means 'gathered threads'—which, in ancient cultures, symbolized the first step in joining life partners."

Christian looked at the bracelet on his wrist and gave Keanu a curious half-smile. "You're making it up."

Keanu shook his head and held up three fingers in the Scouts' Honor sign. Then he pointed at Christian's bracelet and said, "The red symbolizes love, passion, and courage. The blue symbolizes loyalty, trust, and emotional depth." Then he nodded at the bracelet on Jake's wrist. "The green stands for growth, healing, and peace. And the yellow for happiness, joy, and positivity." Then he nodded at both bracelets and added, "The black and white threads of the loose ends where you tied them off represent new beginnings, timeless bonds, and strength." Keanu smiled. "You picked them out for each other, I take it?"

Christian shook his head, but was scarcely aware of it.

Keanu nodded at the bracelets again. "Well, whoever *did* pick them out must have sensed that you guys are meant to be together."

Keanu left them to get another round of beers and check on another table. While he was gone, neither spoke. Jake watched as Christian gazed at his own bracelet, a gleam of bitter nostalgia in his eyes. Jake had enough time to regret the decision to go out tonight—it was probably too soon after their loss—when he noticed the young woman across the street and froze.

She wasn't in the convertible, and she didn't have the cat with her. She was alone on the corner as if waiting for someone to pick her up. To his chagrin, Jake thought she looked like an escort waiting for a john. Jake was heartened when a car pulled to the curb and the young woman waved off the driver without so much as a glance. But she continued to look around with cool anticipation . . . as if waiting for the *right* john.

Jake's heart nearly stopped when her eyes lit on him from across the dark street, and for a second, he could have sworn he smelled the aroma of her perfume—the gypsy water—wafting on the night air, like an intoxicating elixir, calling him to her. He found himself rising from his seat, but stopped short when Christian's voice broke the spell.

" . . . Anyway, you should come over and do *The White Lotus* with us, or at least the Full Moon Party episode. Jake's got the sweet setup over at his place."

Jake looked up to find Keanu standing at their table. Judging by the tone of the conversation, he had been there for a while chatting it up with Christian.

"Serious?" Keanu asked.

"As a heart attack," Christian said. "You're our bro now. We're like the three musketeers. You can be Porthos."

Keanu laughed like he could dig it. "Could I bring a friend along?"

"Fuck yeah," Christian said. "The more the merrier! Is he cool? You seeing him?"

Keanu grinned, tipping a nod at Christian's wrist. "We haven't put a bracelet on it yet, but we're working on it."

Christian said, "What's the holdup? Is he cute?"

"Definitely cute," Keanu said. "Just hasn't come out to his family yet, so we're taking it slow. That's him over there," he added with a nod toward the bartender, a good-looking dark-haired guy with a lean and hard body.

"Oh my God," Christian laughed, "we *are* bros, bro. You've got the same taste as me!"

Keanu nodded, with a wink at Jake. "Lean and chiseled." To Christian, he said, "I've tried it with guys like us, but it's too much muscle in one bed, you know? It's like doing it with myself."

Christian almost choked on his beer with laughter. "Exactly! That's what I told *this* guy!" He mussed Jake's hair, and Jake's cheeks went crimson, which made Christian laugh even harder. "Look at this guy—you'd think *he* was the one who just came out, instead of me!"

Keanu laughed. Jake smiled, still blushing. But his smile faltered when he looked across the street to find the young woman was no longer there.

Christian sipped his beer, and still laughing a little, tagged Jake on the arm and said, "What is it? You look like you just saw a ghost, bro."

Jake shook his head and offered a smile as he took the fresh beer Keanu had brought for him.

They chatted with Keanu for a while, and when he went to take care of other tables, Christian stood and held out a hand to Jake. "Come on," he said.

Jake looked up quizzically. "What? Where?"

"It's a surprise," Christian said. "Come on, before I lose my nerve."

Jake noticed with a measure of surprise that Christian's outstretched hand was shaking a little, and he took it into his own. Christian pulled him up to his feet and headed for the entrance, holding Jake's hand as he led the way inside the bar.

At the edge of the dance floor, Christian chuckled in a wavering voice that sounded nothing like his usual self-assured timbre, "I'm nervous as fuck, dude. Couple more beers, and I won't be. But I don't want to be drunk when we do this."

Jake shook his head slowly when he realized what Christian was up to. "I don't dance—" he began, but before he could finish the statement, Christian pressed a finger to his lips.

"Don't worry. It'll be a slow one. You'll be fine. Just follow my lead."

"How do you know it will be a slow one?"

"Because," Christian said with a sly grin, "I slipped Keanu twenty for the DJ with a request while you were spacing out on us out there on the terrace."

Jake smiled with embarrassment, but he let Christian lead him onto the floor, where they were greeted by the opening chords of Collective Soul's *Adored*.

twenty-five

When they pulled into the driveway, Jake half-expected the night to be over, but Christian didn't head for his house. Instead, he walked Jake to his porch, but didn't follow him up to the door. He stopped at the bottom step, his eyes tentative, like the eyes of a teenager back from his first date, about to ask for a goodnight kiss. He didn't ask for a kiss, though. "Movie?" he said.

Jake nodded and smiled. "Sure." But when he took out his key and unlocked the front door, Christian remained where he was. When Jake looked over his shoulder, Christian looked off, toward his own porch, thoughtfully, and Jake asked, "What?"

Christian looked up at Jake, then down at his shoes, and up again. "I'm gonna want to spend the night," he said softly yet clearly. "I'd say we don't have to do anything, but that would be a lie. I mean, we don't *have* to, but I need to know this isn't just a one-off. I meant what I said to you back there, and I need to know if you feel the same."

Christian was referring to what he'd said to Jake on

the dance floor at The Checkered Skirt. The two of them had been close enough to kiss as they moved slowly to the Collective Soul song. The fingers of Christian's right hand had caressed the bracelet around Jake's left wrist; his lips had brushed Jake's ear when he whispered, "I think I'm falling in love with you." He'd paused briefly and amended, "Scratch that. I *know* I'm falling in love with you."

Christian had told him that he didn't need a response right there on the dance floor. He'd told him that he could think about it, and when he was ready, they could talk. But here in front of Jake's house, with five steps separating them, he needed that response.

"I'm not asking for a commitment," Christian said. "I just want to know if I'm pissing up a rope here." He looked away with a sigh, and his nostrils flared briefly. "That was crude. I didn't mean it that way. I just meant—"

"You're not pissing up a rope," Jake said, with a small smile. "I want you to spend the night." He was about to add, "I want you to spend *more* than just the night," but Christian was already up the steps, one hand on Jake's cheek, his fingers moving back into Jake's hair as he kissed him on the lips, slowly and deeply. Their noses were still touching when their lips parted, and Jake smiled and said, "The neighbors are probably watching."

Christian said, "Fuck 'em, let 'em watch," and kissed Jake again.

When they settled down in front of the TV with a big bowl of popcorn, Christian said he wanted to watch something gay. Jake, whose knowledge of gay cinema was fairly limited for a gay guy, suggested *Brokeback Mountain*, but Christian rolled his eyes and shook his head. "Been there, done that. It was good—OK, *really* good—but I want something hardcore . . . like *The Terminator*."

Jake squinted as if he'd misheard. "*The Terminator*? You're kidding, right?"

Christian laughed his high-pitched laugh. "Come on, dude! *The Terminator* is one of the most homoerotically charged flicks of all time—second only to *Point Break*!"

Jake smiled, waiting for the punchline.

Christian laughed again. "I'm serious. It starts with two naked hot guys coming from the future—who, coincidentally, are a lot like us." He tapped a finger to his chest. "Me, Terminator." He tapped Jake's chest. "You, Kyle Reese." On Jake's dubious look, he chuckled. "OK, I'm not as mega-pumped as Arnold, but you get the picture. And *you* definitely have that tight Kyle Reese bod, lean and hard, and the darkly edgy good-looks."

Jake snorted a laugh. Christian laughed, too.

"Anyway, hear me out. These two hotties come from the future . . . *naked*—did I mention that?"

"I believe you may have," Jake said with a speculative smile.

"One of them is sent to destroy the future, the other to save it. And they spend the whole movie shooting at each other, but mostly missing, other than a few flesh wounds—OK, the Terminator loses an eye and is reduced to an endoskeleton in the climax, but the point is, they keep on going."

"Until Reese blows the Terminator up, and Sarah crushes him in the hydraulic press," Jake interjected.

"True," Christian said, with a light in his eye. "But that doesn't change the dynamic of Reese and the Terminator's bromance."

Jake's eyes narrowed. He still wasn't getting it. "So, the whole movie was just 'foreplay' between Reese and the Terminator?"

"Exactly!" Christian beamed. "It's all a setup for the second movie, when the Terminator returns to protect his kid!"

Jake shook his head, completely lost now. "*His* kid?"

"*Their* kid," Christian said with emphasis. "Reese and the Terminator—the two fathers of John Connor. In the first movie, the Terminator is still in the closet—he's so sexually repressed that the only way he can express his feelings for Reese is by trying to kill him. But when he comes back in the second movie, he's changed and ready to be a father to his and Reese's son. Sarah even says it: 'Of all the would-be fathers who came and went over the years, this thing, this machine, was the only one who measured up. In an insane world, it was the sanest choice.'"

Jake suddenly flashed back on the image of Christian and Nacho watching the Super Kitties on that final day while he'd stood in the arch between the hallway and the living room. The boy had looked so tiny in Christian's lap, encircled safely by those strong arms. Jake could still hear the song, *Best Day Ever*, playing softly at the back of his mind. Could that really only have been yesterday morning?

Christian must have seen something in Jake's eyes because his demeanor suddenly shifted, and he started to say that they didn't have to watch *The Terminator*, that they could do another movie, when Jake said with a smile, "I'm up for it. Let's get our gay on with Skynet."

Christian pulled out his phone to purchase the movie, and raised a brow, "They've got a bundle deal for one and two. Wanna make it a double feature?"

"Hell yeah," Jake said with casual ebullience. "We can't just watch the one where you're shooting blanks from the closet. We gotta see the sequel, where you come out on rainbow wings and proclaim your undying love for Reese."

Clicking the 'buy' button on his phone and shaking his head, Christian grinned smoothly. "You'll see, smartass."

They watched both movies back-to-back. Though thoroughly engrossed in the action, Christian shot a couple of sly glances in Jake's direction during the "gay scenes"—the gayest of all being the shootout at Tech Noir between the two male leads. All the steely gazes, tumbling dives by Reese, rapid-fire sprays from the Terminator's Uzi 9mm, and reloading of weapons tickled Christian pink, and Jake couldn't help agreeing that the whole ballet of bullets *did* sort of come off like something straight out of "The Commando's Guide To Foreplay On The Boudoir Battlefield." But otherwise, their viewing was quiet—*respectful*, Jake thought—in deference to Christian's assertion that the Terminator and Kyle Reese were the joint fathers of John Connor.

The second movie ended shortly after midnight. Jake thought Christian might pick up the thread of their pre-movie conversation—maybe even make a few jokes about the T-1000 *actually* being sent by Skynet to reboot the T-800 unit back to his factory-approved heterosexual mode.

But Christian sat quietly during the entire credit crawl, and Jake was pretty sure why. After the destruction of the T-1000 on the catwalk above the molten steel, Christian had lost all traces of his winking humor. Jake had kept his eyes focused on the screen when the Terminator said there was one more chip to destroy, but he could feel Christian tensing on the sofa beside him. And when the boy started crying and ordered the Terminator not to go, Jake was pretty sure he glimpsed a tear spill down Christian's cheek, and, further, that this display of emotion had nothing to do with the movie.

Christian didn't go back to his house afterward. He headed upstairs with Jake. They took turns in the bath-room, and when Christian came out in his boxers, Jake was already turning down the bed. Christian helped him fold the large, fluffy comforter at the foot of the bed, and the two of them slipped under the top sheet. The heatwave had yet to break, but there was a nice breeze coming through the open window, and neither Jake nor Christian liked sleeping with the air-conditioning on anyway.

For a moment, Jake thought they would both drift off to sleep without a word. Then, from the darkness, Christian spoke. "That was cool. I've never done them back-to-back like that before. Kinda puts the whole story into perspective, you know?"

Jake nodded, but he couldn't tell if Christian could see him by the minimal moonlight peeking through the open sheers, so he said softly, "Yeah, it does."

He waited for a moment, wondering if now was the time to discuss what had happened with Nacho. But before he could speak, Christian shifted gears. "I think I knew I had feelings for you the day you brought over that letter, the one the postman put in your box by accident. It was just some bullshit junk mail, but I didn't throw it out. I tucked it away in a drawer . . . and pulled it out every now and again, thinking of the way you looked on my porch when you rang the bell to return it. I remember exactly what you looked like that day. I used to play that moment over and over in my mind, you at the door with that letter. And sometimes, I would imagine what it would have been like if I'd invited you in for a beer." He paused before going on. "You were wearing those black Doc Marten brogues and those olive trousers, with a white dress shirt—one without buttons to hold down the collar, so one of the collar tips stuck up a little, and it was *so* you, with that tousled hair and your loose tie. And I thought, 'This guy's a teacher? He looks like a student trying to *look* like a teacher!'" The high-pitched laugh came, and Jake smiled bashfully.

"So when did you first know you liked me—and don't say it was when you saw me mowing the lawn shirtless, because that will really tank my opinion of you."

Jake smiled sheepishly. "You've got a great body."

"Yeah, but I won't always have it. One day, I'm gonna get old, and I want to know that you love me for more than just that. So come up with something a little more substantial than my pecs and abs."

"You also have a great ass," Jake joked, attempting to veer the conversation away from where it was obviously headed.

Christian rolled his eyes. "Tell me something I don't know."

Jake considered, even though he knew the precise moment he'd fallen for Christian—the moment he'd understood that Christian was the hero of his story. It had happened outside The Front Grille when Christian had spotted Nacho and called him away from the black car with the tinted windows.

But he didn't say this to Christian. It was too soon, and he didn't want to remind Christian of his loss.

Our loss, Jake corrected himself silently.

He decided to lie and said that his feelings for Christian had dawned at roughly the same time, when he'd found the letter addressed to Christian in his mailbox. This was only a white lie, of course, because, had he not been interested in Christian, he would have simply left the misdirected post in Christian's box and walked away without ringing the bell.

"So we both got struck by the same arrow at the same time," Christian said with a laugh. "A misdirected letter. That's like some hardcore kismet, eh?"

Jake didn't respond. And for a time, it was quiet.

Then, Christian said something completely unexpected. "Did you see her, too? The gypsy chick, across the street, while I was talking with Keanu, did you see her?"

Jake remained silent, but his heart hammered a slow, pounding beat inside his chest.

"She didn't get in anybody's car," Christian said, "if that's what you were wondering." He paused and then continued, almost in a whisper, "She wasn't looking for any of them. She was looking for something else . . . "

Jake remained still. Christian shot a soft breath out of his nose. Though it was dark in the room, and Jake couldn't see him, he knew that Christian's nostrils had flared with disdain upon the exhalation of that breath.

Seconds passed like minutes, and then Christian spoke again in that same near-whisper. "I used to believe that God had a plan, that everything was going to work out the way it was supposed to. I still believed it, even after Marilyn . . . lost the baby." Another exhalation, scarcely audible this time. "But I don't know if I believe it anymore. It's got nothing to do with faith. I have enough faith." He took a steady breath. "I have the faith that I'm gonna find him, and I don't care what the *fuck* God thinks about that. He's *our* son—he came to us, he *chose* us—and I'm going to get him back." He took another breath, and his voice was steady and sure when he asked the only question that mattered. "Are you with me?"

Jake's response wasn't verbal. He reached out in the darkness and laced the fingers of his left hand with the fingers of Christian's right hand, and as he squeezed, the bracelets that Nacho had won for them at the bottle toss game touched.

It was 12:42 AM, and there was still enough time. Somehow, Jake knew this as he slipped out of his boxers, tossed them aside, and climbed on top of Christian. "Do you have faith in us?" he asked, pressing a hand to Christian's bare chest. Christian nodded, and Jake removed his boxers, too, tossing them to the carpet next to his own.

It lasted for several long minutes, but as the seconds of each of those minutes ticked away, Jake felt sure they could still make it. When Christian raised his head and kissed Jake with passion, Jake understood that he wanted to get on top and make it last for a while. But Jake pushed him back onto the pillow—there wasn't time for that; not right now. For now, it was important that Jake remain in control. The midnight hour would soon expire, and with it, all hope would vanish. He knew this as surely as he knew that his love for Christian was true, and so he continued in the rhythm that he'd set. And Christian followed, looking deeply into Jake's eyes as he responded to his every touch, every caress, every kiss.

Jake became distracted only once—when the shadows on their periphery shifted, and the sheers over the open window billowed in the warm breeze, which carried upon it the faint yet distinct scent of gypsy water. He didn't ignore this intrusion, but welcomed it into the circle as he drew Christian closer, and their bodies became one.

When the billowing sheers whispered from the shadows with measured exigency, Jake knew it was time, and he breathlessly whispered, "We have to come now."

Christian nodded; he was already coming, and as he clung to Jake, he whispered, "I love you so much. I love you so much. I love you so . . . "

Jake's body tensed with the final thrust. He wanted to say, "I love you, too," but could only manage an unintelligible groan as he buried his face in the hollow of Christian's neck and kissed his throat.

And when his orgasm was complete, he collapsed onto Christian's broad chest, breathing heavily. For a moment, all he could hear was the sound of their hearts beating in unison. But underneath that crashing twin tidal wave, he could have almost sworn he heard something else . . .

The phantom statement that may or may not have escaped Christian's lips in a breathless whisper sounded like, *"She's here."*

twenty-six

Gods clashed in thunderous battle. Oceans rose to swallow whole continents. Vixens writhed in agonizing throes of passion. Pixies danced in deleterious delight. Angels took wing, furiously fanning the flames of stithy. Demons hissed in strangled sibilants of dissent.

Yet the Parcae, beholden to none (for one day they would reap all and start afresh), turned a blind eye and a deaf ear to the din. Their judgment had already been passed—even before the consecration and consummation—and all three had fallen squarely on the side of life.

Nona spun a thread of beauty and purity. Decima measured a length of grace and wonder. And Morta, most perspicacious of the three, stayed her scissors with calculated patience and rumination . . . while somewhere below two young men, who had defied all odds to meet in the fabled middle-ground of No Man's Land, slept peacefully entwined in a sweet tangle of limbs, dreaming the same dream.

twenty-seven

On the eighth day after the storm that had torn through the idyllic hamlet of Dante's Haven with the vengeance of a scorned demiurge, the heatwave that followed in its wake finally broke, and a cool autumn breeze wafted through Jake Leary's open bedroom window, raising tiny goosebumps on his bare arms and back. He woke naked under the sheet, wanting nothing more than to pull the comforter up from the foot of the bed and burrow into his pillow for a few extra winks of sleep.

But Jake didn't do this. Instead, he reached toward the other side of the bed—Christian's side of the bed—and felt for the warm body he hoped would be there. He wasn't aroused yet, but he *would* be once his hand made contact. He didn't care if the morning started with sex; he just wanted to hold onto someone. He wanted to hold onto Christian.

When his hand found nothing but the cool sheet (not even a warm spot where Christian had recently lain), he opened his eyes and looked at the empty side of the bed.

He lay for a moment, listening for the morning sounds that he'd grown accustomed to over the past week. But nothing came from the kitchen. He was alone in the house.

The bathroom tiles were cold on his bare feet, and after a week of cool morning showers, he ducked his head under the blissfully steamy spray from the showerhead, indulging in the warmth. He wanted to stay longer in the steam-streaked stall, but something inside tugged at him with a mild sense of urgency to get out and get dressed. This first true day of autumn, September 26th, was going to be an important day—he didn't know why, but he felt this inherently—and he didn't want to waste a moment of it languishing in the shower, no matter how good it felt.

He toweled off, dressed, and was downstairs in short order. The kitchen was empty, as he'd expected it would be. But there was a mixing bowl on the counter whose contents looked like pancake batter. He went to the bay window in the breakfast nook and spotted Christian in the driveway next door. At once, a wave of tendrils raced along his arms, and his stomach did a somersault. It was a sensation he hadn't felt since he was fourteen and had his first crush on a boy named Matt Hasney, who had gone on to become a Secret Service agent and had received a Purple Heart for injuries sustained while protecting the youngest son of the President from a foreign assassin.

Matt had been blond, blue-eyed, and fairly well-built for a fourteen-year-old, and Jake had been head over heels for him. They had been friends all through their freshman year of high school; Jake had even tutored Matt in Algebra. Nothing ever happened between them, and the initial sensation of near-debilitating euphoria generally passed quickly, leaving a warm feeling of comfort whenever he and Matt spent time together. But Jake had never forgotten the way his stomach did acrobatics every time he first encountered Matt after being away from him for more than a few days.

He felt that same sensation now as he watched Christian, down on one knee at the back of his Jeep. At first, Jake wasn't sure what Christian was doing—all he could tell was that he looked very focused and diligent. It wasn't until Christian stood with the curled rectangular sheet sticking to the fingers of his hand that Jake understood. Christian crumpled the bumper sticker and pitched it into the dumpster before coming inside. He greeted Jake with a smile and a kiss on the lips before heading to the sink to wash his hands.

Jake didn't say anything about what he'd just seen in the driveway. But Christian did. Toweling off his hands, he muttered clearly, "I'm tired of all the fuckin' hate." And then, he started breakfast.

When Jake asked if there was anything he could do to help, Christian grinned as if he'd heard a mildly funny joke.

"Hey," Jake said, with a wavering smile, "I think I can whip a couple of eggs."

That brought the laughter, and as Christian took up the mixing bowl of batter and began stirring, he said, "I'll never boss you around in the bedroom or anywhere else—*except* for the kitchen. I solemnly swear it. Fair enough?"

Christian was still grinning, but Jake suspected that he was serious and nodded. Marc had wanted control of the kitchen and everything else, so this one concession seemed like a small sacrifice—and, in truth, Jake really didn't like cooking anyway. But his acquiescence was so sweet that

Christian felt a little guilty and told him that there wasn't much left to do.

"I already made the batter while you were sleeping—it's been resting for an hour now and should be perfect. But you can help by making the coffee and pouring the orange juice."

Jake smiled. "So I can be the sous chef?"

The high-pitched laugh came again, with an eye roll this time. "Let's not get the cart before the horse. Baby steps first. For now, you can be the 'prep cook,' so chop-chop before I demote you to 'porter.'"

The batter didn't turn out to be for pancakes. Christian served up stacks of light crêpes with delicate centers and crispy edges, topped with fresh strawberry slices, whole blackberries, and fine lines of maple syrup drizzle. Like everything Christian made in the kitchen, the meal was delicious, prompting Jake to ask why Christian didn't have his own restaurant.

Christian found this amusing. "I cook to relax," he said. "If I did it for a living, I think it would defeat the purpose." And with a wink, he added, "I'm comfortable managing the accounts of rich pricks with more disposable cash than they know what to do with. At least, for now, I am. If I get bored, my teaching certificate's still current—I could always join you in the trenches."

Jake wasn't exactly a teacher. He occasionally subbed for a few classes at his alma mater while former professors were on break. But his occupation was in computer engineering at Microsoft, which paid very well and allowed him the flexibility to work from home, which he often did. Jake suspected Christian already knew this and just liked calling him "Teach."

This was cool by Jake; he not only liked the nickname, but anticipated it coming up in the bedroom over time as they grew close enough to engage in some role-play.

"What are you smiling about?" Christian inquired with a sly smile of his own, causing Jake to blush at Christian's canny ability to seemingly read his thoughts. Before Jake could respond, Christian said, "If it's sex, it'll have to wait . . . at least until tonight, when, I guarantee you, I'm gonna hound your ass until you give it to me in the shower again. Is that too forward too soon?" Jake shook his head, grinning. "Good. I'm newly liberated, and I have a lot of catching up to do. But if it gets to be too much, just slap my nose or something, and I'll back off like a dog."

But Jake didn't want him to back off—certainly not after last night. He'd never felt such passion before and could hardly wait to go there again.

"But," Christian said, scooping the last forkful of crêpes off his plate, "it's gonna have to wait because today, I want to repair that fence, and it's gonna be a full day's work."

Jake thought about this and said, "Or we could just leave it down . . . "

Christian made a face. "What if we don't like the new neighbors? You know what they say about good fences." He smiled. Then, almost instantly, his smile faltered, and he shook his head. "That was stupid. I'm sorry. I didn't mean to push like that. I just—"

Jake cut him off, knowing in his heart that, given the insane week they'd just shared, it was the sanest choice.

"You know what?" Jake said, with a single arched brow. "I think we should go fix that fence."

twenty-eight

It didn't take as long to repair the fence as they'd thought it would. Finding matching pickets to fill the section smashed by the fallen tree was the trickiest bit and had taken all of the morning and part of the afternoon. They went to five different big box stores before finally locating a lumber mill, where an old-timer was able to replicate the size and shape of the posts and pickets to Jake's precise specifications. Christian chuckled on their way out of the store, "Dude, you are so *anal!* I can't believe that old guy trimmed those pickets to your exact measurements! Those beer-bellies at The Depot would have laughed you out of the store and told you to trim them down yourself . . . and then probably let you know just where you could stick 'em."

Christian laughed. Jake flushed.

"It's all good. I'm cool with anal guys." He shot Jake a look with a grin. "You know what I mean. Get your mind out of the gutter, bitch." And he laughed again.

They spent the rest of the afternoon filling in the fifteen-foot section of the demolished fence. This was the area where Christian ceded control to Jake, who performed precise calculations and measurements to ensure the new pickets aligned perfectly with the old ones.

When they were done, they stood back to admire their work, and Christian said with a smile, "Math over muscle."

He wasn't kidding; he was impressed with the even row of pickets that, once primed and covered with a fresh coat of paint, would be indistinguishable from the rest of the fence. He looked at the sky and said, "Looks like it's gonna be a clear night. We can get the priming done tomorrow morning, and the first coat of paint in the afternoon." He rubbed his stomach. "For now, let's get cleaned up and hit that pasta place. I'm starving."

They showered in their separate dwellings (both fully aware that a "chance encounter" at this point would only delay dinner) and then met at Christian's Jeep in the driveway. The wait for a table at the little Italian restaurant was going to be a half-hour or more, and with their stomachs grumbling, they decided on a change of venue and went to The Grille instead.

They were going to take a table and dine in, but Christian seemed antsy, as if there was some other place he needed to be, so when their server came, Jake suggested they order burgers and eat them on The Checkered Skirt's patio with a couple of cold ones.

Christian made a face and gestured at the bar as if Jake were dense. "They've got beer here, dude."

"I know," Jake said, and added with a sheepish smile, "but it tastes better when Keanu brings it."

Christian shook his head with a laugh, but his edginess evaporated, and he nodded agreeably. The Skirt seemed precisely the place to be tonight.

Keanu greeted them with a big smile and told them it was OK to bring the food inside. Jake shook his head like it was all good. Somehow, he knew that they needed to be on the patio this evening, and further, that they needed to be at their usual table, close to the sidewalk.

It was a pleasant, quiet meal, with a nice breeze coming off the lake that felt refreshing after the stifling heat over the past seven days. In the dawn of autumn, with the leaves soon to be turning and then falling before the winter's sleep, Jake felt oddly awake, as if impending life was in the air, stirring scattered leaves across the pavement as it breathed its first breath all around him. And when he looked across the table, he felt sure it was the same for Christian. Though he looked like a boy of summer, with his blond hair, blue eyes, and buffed body, Jake felt that, at least for this night, at this hour, Christian was an autumn person . . . or at least was on the precipice of becoming one.

I would have been a good dad.

Jake believed this; he believed it with all his heart. Christian was ready to embrace the autumn—or maturity—of his life. And he had enough faith to do it.

But Jake was still unsure about himself. Was he ready to take that same leap of faith?

The question became moot when, shortly after they finished their meal, the aleatoric hand of fate returned and made the decision for both of them. Whether they were ready or not, autumn had arrived and was beckoning with exigency.

Christian spotted the girl first. She had appeared at the gate as if out of thin air. She was alone and wrapped in a bedsheet. When they had seen her the night before, she had been trim in her blue dress and high heels, but now she was hunched over and clutched the gate rail with one hand while holding the considerable swell of her belly with the other, in obvious pain.

Christian sprang from his seat, hurdling the gate in a single bound. He made it just in time to catch her as she fell forward and into his arms. She spoke in her native tongue, but Christian didn't need Jake to interpret. The message was clear.

"Бепиг схьадогӀуш ду. (*The Baby is coming*)."

Keanu broke off in the middle of taking an order at a nearby table and called to Christian, "Is that the woman you were looking for? Is she OK?"

Christian nodded. "Call the hospital. Tell them we're on our way. The baby is coming."

Jake was on the sidewalk now, taking the keys from Christian and opening the Jeep's back door. Cradling the girl in his arms, Christian carried her to the Jeep and carefully placed her in the backseat. He took the keys from Jake and said, "You sit with her. I'll drive." He shot a glance at Keanu on his way around the car and to the driver's seat. Keanu was already on his mobile phone. He gave Christian a thumbs-up as he waited for the hospital's operator to pick up.

In the backseat, Jake held the young woman's hand. Her grip was so tight, it almost hurt, but he assumed it was a good sign that she still had strength. She was sweating profusely with each contraction—at least Jake hoped they were contractions and not something more serious. He told her it was OK, that Christian would get them to the hospital in no time, and everything would be all right.

The girl was speaking through clipped breaths and painful contractions. It was all coming out so rapidly that it took a moment for Jake to realize she was not speaking in English. But this didn't matter, because all he could hear was what she had said to him the night they'd first met . . .

He is gypsy from Ukraine—but will be born in 'Merica, so to be 'Merican.

Not *was* born in America, past tense. But *will be* born in America, as if the boy had not yet come into existence.

Also Chechen because one father Chechen, and other 'Merican. But mother is Ukrainian gypsy and smart like 'Merican, so move him here before is conceive.

You are Ashkenazi; boy is same.

Mother is die young.

Like you, left with father to raise.

Jake's father had been primarily Irish and Italian. But his mother had been an Ashkenazi Jew, and her parents had been Chechen immigrants.

The young woman bit back a scream as Christian rounded a corner at breakneck pace. Then, she looked up into Jake's eyes and spoke in her broken English. "Good match. Both handsome. You marry, keep boy."

Though the pain was severe, she managed a smile. Jake returned the smile, but his rational mind was crying out, *This can't be real, this can't be real.*

The Jeep jerked to a stop in front of the emergency entrance, and Christian was out of the driver's seat, opening the back door, and taking the girl into his arms. As her hand slid from Jake's, her fingertips grazed the bracelet on his wrist, and then she was leaning into Christian's shoulder as he raced through the open doors of the ER, calling out, "Can we get some help, please? This woman is having a baby right now."

twenty-nine

In a curtained room off the main corridor, Christian held the girl's hand and asked the nurse, "Can you give her something for the pain?"

"I'm afraid that's the doctor's call," the nurse said. But her eyes said it was doubtful the girl could have anything until after the baby was born.

Christian looked back at the girl and gave her hand a gentle squeeze. "You just hold on tightly. And if you need to, you squeeze my hand as hard as you can and look into my eyes, OK?"

She nodded, squeezing his hand.

Christian smiled reassuringly and asked softly, "What's your name?"

"Sabine," the girl said.

"Sabine," Christian repeated as if it were the sweetest name he'd ever heard, and it was. Tears were standing in his eyes, but they did not fall. He held them back bravely. "That's a beautiful name."

She touched her stomach. "He is Dzhokhar, but will not like, so you give name he like."

"*You* can give it to him," Christian said gently. "Once he comes, you can give it to him."

"No," the girl said. She was smiling, but her eyes were fading. "He is life now. Your son." She nodded toward Jake with effort. "His son. Make baby with me under shadow of moon. Omen. Good omen. New moon, new life."

Christian said, "It's not the new moon yet."

Sabine's smile was wan, but her eyes were sure. "It will be . . . soon . . . good men, both raise together. Two dads . . . is legal now . . . long, happy life."

"We can all do it together. You can stay with us. We'll take care of you and the baby." Christian's voice trembled now, and a tear escaped. It rolled down his cheek, and Sabine gently brushed it with her thumb and clasped it in her hand, close to the Saint Jude medallion around her neck.

"For luck," she said with a smile. "For hope." Her smile was cut off instantly by a sudden stabbing pain in her side. "Baby is come now." She squeezed Christian's hand as she gazed into his eyes. "Your son. Looks more like him," she said, with a nod toward Jake, "but strong like you. But not with the muscles. With the heart." She pressed her fingers against Christian's chest. "In here. Like White Wolf." She pressed harder. "Strong. You will protect him."

"And you, too," Christian said bravely.

She made a wavering gesture with her hand, the same as Nacho had done, and smiled. "We'll see."

The doctor came then, and things happened quickly.

Too quickly.

167

A team was called in, and the doctor told them that Sabine was being taken to Delivery. Christian tried to go with, but the nurse, a stout woman in her late fifties, told him that he would have to wait. Christian was about to say that he was the baby's father, but Sabine smiled and said to the nurse, "Is OK. He is nervous papa." And to Christian she said, "You stay. Baby come soon. He will be OK. You will take care of him."

The baby drew his first breath exactly one minute and fifty-three seconds before the mother drew her last. She wasn't able to hold him. But she heard him crying and knew that he was alive and weighed 3.42 kg, which was a healthy weight and, cumulatively, a very lucky number—3, 4, 2, equaling 9, a number which stood for fruition and completion. From head to toe, he was 49.9 cm and would be tall like his fathers. And handsome, too.

She knew all of this when the team raced in with the crash cart, and the bright light above her eyes was no longer coming from the LED bulb above the operating theatre.

thirty

The doctor was young and fit. The name stitched into his scrubs was EDWARD SOON, MD. A Pacific Islander, like Keanu, Dr. Soon looked like he'd be more comfortable in boardshorts catching waves than in scrubs delivering babies. His surgical mask was pulled down from his face and hung loose around his neck. He wore the tired expression of someone deep into a double shift on a grueling day. He stood facing the two men but addressed Jake. "Are you the father?"

"We both are," Christian said before Jake could respond. His voice sounded thick.

Jake said, "She was our surrogate."

The doctor nodded. "Well, they'll need a pre-birth order or a DNA test to establish parentage before they can release the baby to you."

Christian's eyes hardened. "He's our son."

The doctor nodded again. "I understand that, sir. It's just a matter of verifying things for legal purposes. If the mother was, as you say, your surrogate, all you'll need is the pre-birth order."

Christian's eyes narrowed. "You think we're lying?"

The doctor shook his head. "No, sir, I'm not suggesting anything of the kind. I'm just telling you that we can't release a newborn to—"

"*We* brought her *in* here," Christian said, and was about to add, "What do you think, we just picked her up on the street and decided to adopt her baby after she died?" But he stopped himself.

"I understand that, sir," the doctor said in that same calm tone, which had zero calming effect on Christian. "But we have to follow hospital protocol."

Jake saw how the situation could easily escalate, and said, "Can we just take the DNA test? How long would that take?"

"The swab won't take long. We can do that right now. The results usually take twenty-four to forty-eight hours."

"Do you send them out to a lab?" Jake asked.

"Not typically. We have a gen lab on premises."

"Then, why does it take so long?" Christian interjected, his eyes steely again.

Dr. Soon nodded as if this was a reasonable question, and said, "Look, the baby is going to be here for a couple of days, regardless, which is standard in cases like this, where the mother . . . is no longer there to nurse the child. He'll be given formula, possibly even breast milk from a surrogate, and the nurse will go over specific care instructions with you before you take him home. They'll have the DNA test results before he's ready for discharge."

Christian's posture relaxed, but his eyes remained steely.

Jake asked, "When can we take the test?"

"Right now, if you like," the doctor said. "The lab is on the third floor. Just tell them I sent you, and they'll take care of everything."

Jake nodded, ready to thank the doctor, but Christian shook his head, his eyes still on the man who looked more like a surfer than a surgeon. "No. I want you to do it."

Dr. Soon smiled gently and said, "It's just a cheek swab. You'll be in and out in no time, and then you can see your son."

"Then it shouldn't be a problem for you to do it," Christian said. "I take it you're qualified."

Dr. Soon met Christian's unflinching gaze in kind, and for a moment, Jake thought they looked like Terminators— the T-800 models, ready to engage in combat.

Jake was about to intercede when something passed between Christian and the doctor, the same silent code that had passed between Christian and Keanu when they'd first met at The Checkered Skirt, and for a strange moment, Jake half-expected them to exchange the secret handshake that he had yet to master.

But this didn't happen. Instead, Edward Soon, MD, simply gestured toward the elevator.

In the lab, the doctor washed his hands and put on a pair of surgical gloves before getting the sanitary-wrapped swab. "OK, gentleman, who are we swabbing?"

Jake momentarily froze. It hadn't occurred to him which of them would need to be tested. They had both been there at the moment of conception, but only one of them could be the biological father, right? The rational side of his brain seemed to cry this out. But could anything that had happened over the past week be considered rational, from the first appearance of the boy at the age of eighteen to the gradual decrease in his age until he was no longer there? Could two men make love and conceive a child with a woman who wasn't even present?

But she was *there*, some part of Jake's mind cried out. She had entered the room when the sheers had billowed in the warm breeze. He had smelled the aroma of her intoxicating perfume. He had felt her gentle touch guiding him in as he looked into Christian's eyes.

Still, that rational part of his brain resisted the notion. Even if all that had preceded this outcome was true, could any woman—even one as cannily sibylline as Sabine—conceive and carry a baby to full term in less than twenty-four hours?

All of these questions passed through Jake's mind in a split second, but he was still puzzling over the possible answers when Christian stepped in and said, "Test both of us." On the doctor's raised brow, he said, "We both submitted samples. We don't know which one took."

He was lying, and of course, Jake knew it. But the doctor didn't question his story. He simply nodded and said, "OK. Who's first?"

Jake sat on the exam table and opened his mouth. After the swabbing was done, Christian did the same, sitting calmly while Dr. Soon swabbed him. Jake watched the procedure, recalling how easily and convincingly Christian had lied to Keanu about their names that first night at The Checkered Skirt, and couldn't help thinking, *This is a pissing contest between frat boys.* He expected that Christian already knew how the tests would turn out. The only question was, how would Dr. Edward Soon deal with those results once they came in?

It was this thought that led Jake to believe that Christian hadn't arbitrarily insisted on Dr. Soon personally conducting the swabbing, that the choice of Edward Soon, "brother of the secret handshake" (whether or not he'd shared said handshake with Christian on this particular night) and member of "the order of hot surfers," had been a deliberately calculated gambit on Christian's part.

They went up to the maternity ward, and though there were nine babies lined up in plastic cribs, four of them wrapped in blue blankets, Christian's eyes immediately homed in on the one sleeping peacefully in the middle.

He's our son—he came to us, he chose us—and I'm going to get him back. Are you with me?

Standing next to Christian and looking through the observation room window at their baby, Jake realized that he didn't care how it had come to pass. He nodded silently and took Christian's hand, squeezing it. Christian squeezed back, and their bracelets touched.

They stood there for a brief while before a nurse came and asked which one was theirs. When Christian nodded toward the center crib, the nurse asked, "Would you like to hold him?"

Christian nodded again, and when both he and Jake were garbed in gowns and scrub caps, the nurse placed the baby into Christian's arms. Jake stood at Christian's side, and as they gazed down at the sleeping baby, the nurse said, "He has your birthmark, Dad." She nodded at Christian's arm. "I noticed it when you were putting on your gown." She smiled warmly. "His looks just like it—dot with a backward comma below it. Same arm too."

Christian didn't need to look. He knew the birthmark would be there.

When the nurse asked if they had decided on a name yet. Christian nodded and said softly, "Lochlan . . . Lochy."

"That's a beautiful name," the nurse said, and looking between Jake and Christian, she asked, "Who picked it?"

A tear rolled down Christian's cheek and fell gently on the baby's hand. "He did."

The nurse smiled, assuming that Christian was referring to Jake. But Jake knew better; he had been there when the boy had decided he wanted a new name.

You want to be Lochy now? Christian had asked at the table outside the mini golf course.

Not now. Later, the boy had signed.

OK, buddy. You let us know when you want the name change to go into effect, Christian had replied with a smile.

Jake looked at the teardrop on the tiny hand—beaded like a droplet from a baptism—and realized with sudden limpidity that, here in this peaceful moment, "later" had finally arrived.

thirty-one

The DNA tests came in the following day, but Dr. Soon didn't discuss the results with the two fathers until after he'd conducted a second test. He did this with new samples he'd collected from both men on their overnight stay in the maternity waiting room, where Jake slept while Christian remained like a sentry guarding the boy. Dr. Soon conducted the new tests on his own, without the assistance of a pathologist.

When they met in a small office down the hall from the maternity ward, Edward Soon produced a folder and set it on the desk. He did not mince words, but cut straight to the point.

"These are the results of both tests, the one that was conducted by pathology, and the one that I personally oversaw last night. And for reasons I can't explain, they're both identical. Also, for reasons I can't explain, I believe you both already know the results of these tests." He paused before going on. "I suppose I could order an autopsy on the mother, since I'm guessing that neither of you has any paperwork to back up your claim of surrogacy. And I suppose that given the ... unusual outcome of these tests—and that's putting it mildly—I would have no problem getting a judge to sign that order. But to what end? What would I find that I don't already know ... as unbelievable as what I know is?"

Both Christian and Jake remained silent.

Dr. Soon took out the sheets of paper and laid them on the desk in two neat piles. He tapped the first and looked at Jake. "These results are identical. Both indicate that you're the father, at 99.99%." He tapped the other set of papers and looked at Christian. "These results are the same. Both place you at a 99.99% match to be the father."

Christian's nostrils flared, but still, he didn't speak. He simply met Edward Soon's gaze without flinching. Jake wasn't sure he could do that, and so, he asked, peremptorily, "Didn't I read something about two guys who both tested the same on a paternity case back in the early 2000s?"

Edward nodded. "The Miller brothers. But they were identical twins. Are you two related?"

Jake shook his head. He thought of asking how they had solved the paternity issue over the Miller case—he couldn't recall if the article he'd read had come to a definitive conclusion on the matter. But he figured it would be better not to head down a path that could lead to further questions and testing.

Edward released a breath, and Jake was struck by how similar it was to Christian's sigh, the one that signaled he was about to give up. For a moment, Jake allowed himself to feel something close to hope. But then Edward spoke again.

"I've got to be honest, guys. I'm baffled. I've never seen

anything like this in all my years. You two aren't even the same blood type—I ran it on your second swab, just to be sure. The variations in your DNA are unique. And yet you both make a perfect match with the baby."

Jake tried again. "Yeah, but isn't all human DNA 99.9% identical?"

"That's true," said Edward, "But we're not looking at that larger percentage. What we look for is in that remaining 0.1% that makes each individual unique. And in that 0.1%, you both form a near-perfect match for the baby." He sighed again. "Like I said, I've never seen anything like this in all my years."

Christian finally spoke up. "How long have you been a doctor?"

"Nine years."

"You don't look that old."

Edward shrugged. "Good genes."

"So, what're you, thirty-six?"

"Thirty-seven," Edward replied.

Christian nodded, with an appraising look, and Jake had just enough time to wonder whether what he was witnessing was secret bro-code speak when Christian hit Edward Soon with what seemed to Jake a shocking question. "Are you in or out?"

For a moment, Jake thought Christian was asking if the doctor was willing to lie for them and sweep the issue of paternity under the carpet, and a thin line of perspiration broke along his back.

Edward didn't offer a response to Christian's question, but he didn't seem perturbed by it, either.

Christian went on. "Are you married?"

Again, Edward didn't respond, and his calm gaze offered no indication that Christian had struck a chord. But his thumb found the ring on the third finger of his left hand and rocked it slightly.

"You guys have kids?"

Edward said, "Two boys."

"You adopt or use a surrogate?"

For Jake, it was like watching a high-stakes poker hand, waiting to see which player would fold first.

A long moment of silence passed between the two men, during which neither seemed to blink while Jake sweated bullets.

Jake's poker analogy turned out to be an astute one because, in the end, Edward released a light sigh and, placing a hand between the two stacks of paper on his desk, said, "I'm going to put one of these results in your file, and I'm going to give the other one to you guys. Do you have any preference for which becomes official?"

Christian shook his head.

It didn't matter. It was just a piece of paper.

The only thing that mattered was that the baby was coming home with him and Jake.

epilogue

The baby remained in hospital for three days, during which the nurses gave the new fathers a crash course in the care of a newborn. Both learned quickly, and by the third day, they knew how to properly hold the baby, change diapers, warm and serve formula, burp him when he became gassy, and bathe him with a sponge. They also learned the importance of double-dressing to keep the baby warm in colder weather, and how to adjust the layers accordingly to prevent overheating. They had each taken turns staying with him while the other returned home to shower and change clothes. On the second day, Jake took longer to get back to the hospital's maternity ward, but Christian was so enamored with the child that he scarcely noticed his partner's prolonged absence.

Both fathers and son were the darlings of the maternity ward, charming doctors, nurses, and other staff members alike. Dr. Soon came daily to check on the baby's progress, and by his smiling reaction to the newborn and his dads, Jake felt Edward was comfortable with his decision to lay to rest the unusual circumstances surrounding the baby's birth. He even recommended a top pediatrician: his spouse, Dr. Cameron Spencer. Christian took the proffered card, and when he raised a brow at the gender-neutral first name, Edward smiled with a wink and said, "I guess you'll just have to wait until your first appointment for the 'gender reveal.'"

They left the hospital as an official family on the morning of September 30. It was a crisp, sunny day, and Christian sat in the back seat, with the baby next to him, curled comfortably into his carrier under a layer of warm blankets. Jake couldn't help glancing into the rear-view mirror several times as he drove them home, and every time he saw Christian looking down at the sleeping baby, his heart swelled with a feeling so powerful that he felt it might explode at any moment and send him skyward in a shower of brilliant light.

Jake pulled the Jeep into Christian's driveway and killed the engine. Christian got out and unstrapped the carrier, but didn't go to his house. Instead, he headed around the recently repaired fence and went straight for Jake's porch. As Jake unlocked and opened the door, Christian said, "I guess I'll need a set of keys."

Jake nodded. There was a spare set on the counter in the kitchen—one for the front and back doors, and one for the garage. He'd put them there when he'd come back from the hospital to clean up and get things ready for the baby's homecoming.

Christian smiled when he saw the new playpen and matching changing station in the living room. "Somebody's been busy. That why you were gone so long yesterday?"

"I just wanted things to be ready. I don't expect he's ready for the playpen yet—I think one of the nurses said six to nine months, when he becomes mobile. Unless . . . " Jake let the statement hang there. He couldn't finish it.

Christian didn't need him to finish. He said, "That's not going to happen. He's going to grow normally now." On Jake's hopeful look, he said, "I know it. I can feel it. Remember, I'm the one with the faith here, so you're just gonna have to trust me on this one."

And Christian turned out to be right.

On Baby Lochy's first visit to the pediatrician, five days after his release from the hospital, he received a clean bill of health. A month after that, Dr. Spencer said his growth was perfectly normal. By six months, the growth rate was normal as well, and the doctor had only one concern. While the baby was responsive to his name and other sounds, he didn't vocalize his feelings through crying or laughter. Instead, he expressed his feelings through facial expressions and hand gestures. There was no problem with his respiratory system, larynx, or vocal cords—he could make sounds, like cooing and gurgling, and he passed his hearing tests with flying colors. But for reasons unknown, he embraced only non-verbal forms of communication.

Dr. Spencer didn't feel this required immediate attention, but asked that they monitor Lochy's development and keep a journal in case further testing was needed in the future.

Jake kept the journal, as the doctor suggested, and Christian, who had no problem with this, began working with the infant on sign language, which Lochy picked up nicely. At eight months, his signing had become proficient enough to communicate basic needs. At three years, he was signing at the level of a seven-year-old, and by his fifth birthday, he was reading and writing at a fourth-grade level. Though his acumen was well advanced for his age, his body, to Jake's relief, continued to grow at the normal pace for a child.

But all of that came later.

For now, they were content to start their new life together. Christian brought over the crib from next door and set it up in the master bedroom. They would eventually move it once the guest room was converted into a nursery. But that was months away. At this early stage, they both wanted the baby close by.

When Christian finished setting up the crib, they had a light lunch, and later, they ordered out for pizza and ate it while watching a movie with the baby asleep on the sofa between them. And when Lochy woke for one of his many feedings, they paused the movie and Christian warmed the formula while Jake carried the baby around the living room in his arms.

This would become a pattern over time, with Jake and Christian taking turns—one preparing the formula while the other did the feeding. They would take turns with diaper changes as well. And when the "special deliveries" came, they would be greeted by Christian's high-pitched laugh and a cry of, "Whew! Lochy socky!" or when he peed, "Lochy *sake!*" (Both sounded like "socky" to Jake, but Christian said there was a subtle difference, and Jake never argued the point.) And always, Christian would say, "What did you eat, buddy, a skunk? That one's gonna linger!"

When the movie was over, the baby was fast asleep on Christian's chest, and he carried him up to bed, while Jake cleaned up the dinner mess and loaded the dishwasher. He didn't set it going; he would do that the following evening after it was loaded with the dishes from breakfast, lunch, and dinner. He just shut off the lights and headed for the hall.

He was halfway up the stairs when he thought he heard a sound and stopped. He listened for a second, thinking he'd only imagined the sound. But then it came again. Faint yet unmistakable, it sounded like a baby.

Jake looked up the stairs where Christian had gone with Lochy. The light in the master bedroom glowed on its dimmest setting.

When the sound from outside came again, it was accompanied by another sound. Soft scratching.

Jake went down to the foyer and opened the front door. The patchy cat with the heterochromatic eyes was there. He looked up at Jake, uttered a single plaintive cry, and Jake opened the screen door. The cat stepped in, affording Jake a cursory glance before heading straight up the stairs.

Jake followed and found the cat in the master bedroom, where Christian and the baby lay asleep in the big bed. The cat leapt gracefully onto the bed and, with silent precision, proceeded toward the sleeping baby, whom he sniffed with judicious care. This took a moment, but when the cat was satisfied that he had, indeed, found the right place, he went to the foot of the bed and curled up comfortably.

As Jake stood in the doorway, looking at Christian and the baby in peaceful slumber (with the cat curled up like a sentinel on the folded afghan near the footboard, eyes drawn to sleepy slits yet watchful and ready), he felt a calming sense of relief, peace, and love—for the boy, for Christian, for all of them together under the same roof again.

There had been a time, and not long ago, that Jake would have needed answers—perhaps even demanded them. His entire life had been driven by rational thought and a predisposition toward problem-solving. Even as a boy, it had been this way. He'd loved puzzles and video games. But he wasn't like other boys whose only concern was with winning. In fact, Jake didn't mind losing at all, as long as, when the game was over, he could examine what had brought about his defeat, what moves he could have made to better his performance, and possibly even win the next time. He supposed this was why he went on to study engineering in college and why he was inexorably drawn to computer engineering: the desire to find out precisely what made things tick and put those things in proper order.

But now, he wasn't so sure that his innate desire for answers and order mattered to him anymore. Looking at the two people who mattered to him more than anything else in the world, Jake suddenly felt that a bit of *dis*order might be in order. And maybe all you needed to achieve that disorder was a little faith.

He stripped to his boxers, turned out the light, and climbed into bed. By the light of the moon peeking through the window, he looked at his son and the man he would spend the rest of his life with. He still didn't understand how or why it had happened. But he was grateful, and for once in his life, he didn't mind not having the answer. He was content to let the mystery remain a mystery.

He reconciled this by reasoning that, after all, life itself was a mystery.